WELCOME TO HOLYHELL

MATH BIRD

McSnowell Books

A McSnowel Book

First published by All Due Respect Books, 2018
This edition published by McSnowell Books, 2021

Copyright © 2021 by Math Bird

For Yan

PROLOGUE

Someone had sprayed over the W with an H, so the sign said *Welcome to HolyHell*. As Bowen waited at the lights, he wondered who was responsible: some drunk, the town fool, or the bunch of halfwits in the orange Ford Capri behind him. He'd cut them up on the dual carriageway. They beeped him; he gave them the finger, and they'd been tailgating him ever since.

When the lights changed, Bowen made a left, then slammed down on the brakes. The Ford Capri did the same, almost crashing into him. Bowen jumped out of his car and marched over to the driver's window. The kid behind the wheel just stared at him. His mates did the same. Who could blame them? He got that a lot. Bowen was a scary-looking man.

Bowen wiped the sweat from his brow. Hell, it was hot. According to the newspapers, 1976 was the hottest summer since records began. He rested on his haunches and signalled for the kid to wind down the window. He looked the kid in the eye. 'What's your problem?'

The kid glanced over his shoulder and grinned, then fixed Bowen with a stare. 'That's what I was gonna ask you.'

Bowen shook his head and sighed. 'I'm going to make this easy for you. You and your friends apologise, and we'll say no more about it.'

One kid sitting in the back, a long-haired, pasty-faced runt with bad acne, leaned forward. 'Why should we? You started it.'

Bowen reached through the window and opened the car door. He leaned forward and poked the kid in the eye. 'That's why, and if any of you other arse-bandits have anything else to say, I'd think twice about it if I were you because I can give you a load of reasons.'

None of them said a word. The only sound came from the kid in the back, whimpering, telling the world he'd been blinded.

'You'll be fine,' Bowen said. 'I barely touched you; hurts, doesn't it?' He clicked his fingers at the pack of Woodbines on the dashboard. 'Pass 'em to me.'

Without protest, the kid in the driving seat did as he was told. Bowen took out a cigarette, popped it in his mouth, then slipped the pack into his pocket. He nodded at the box of matches. The kid took one out and struck it, his hand shaking as he gave Bowen a light. Bowen took a deep drag and blew the smoke into the car. 'Let's have no more fannying about. Think of this as a friendly warning.'

Bowen stood and got back into his car, watching from the rearview mirror until the kids drove from sight. He smoked his cigarette down to the stump, then flicked it out the window. He took no heed of the warnings; he was more than happy to start a fire.

God, he was tired. Driving up to this northeast corner of Wales took over six hours. When he crossed the border, he felt anxious. He hadn't felt like this for years, and the memories came flooding back.

He took a deep breath and stared at the butcher's shop opposite. In all these years, it hadn't changed: a big, rusty padlock on the door, the window frames still painted black. Hell, he could almost smell the sawdust on the floor to soak up the blood. The pub on his right appeared stuck in a time warp too. The Pig and Whistle was one of his old haunts. He drank his first pint there.

Bowen licked the dryness from his lips. All these memories made a man thirsty.

THE PIG and Whistle was dead. But what could you expect for a Monday night? With his briefcase on his lap, Bowen sat by the window watching his car because it was parked on a double yellow. Not that anyone would ask him to move it, especially at this time. He necked down his pint. The cackling laughter behind him grated on his nerves. He should move on, but they kept a good pint here and now he'd a taste for it. He gripped the handle of his briefcase, stood up, walked over to the bar and ordered another.

He sensed the woman on the barstool next to him staring. When he glanced at her, her eyes fixed on his. He said nothing, just flashed her a smile. She looked in her early thirties but was probably younger. She wasn't bad looking to be fair, busty and tanned, her long bleached hair already showing at the roots. She wore tight denim shorts and a bright yellow top, its laced front showing plenty of cleavage. She held her cigarette as if she owned the place. Probably came here every night.

'Just finished work, have ya?' she said.

'Why do you ask?'

She took a drag on her cigarette and nodded at the brief-case. 'You can leave it on your seat, you know. No one here will steal it.'

She was drunk. It still didn't give her an excuse, and Bowen gave her a look which told her to mind her own business. It seemed to do the trick, causing her to pull a face then turn towards the guy on her left.

The barman handed Bowen his pint. 'That's thirty-two pence, mate.'

Bowen gave him fifty pence, told him to keep the change. At least he'd found one good thing about being back. In some clubs down south, a pint would cost him a quid. He held the thought as he walked back to his seat and slumped into his chair.

Bowen put his pint down on the table, rested the brief-case on his lap, then lit a cigarette. He took a deep drag and blew the smoke up at the ceiling. It felt strange sitting there in his old haunt, almost as though he'd never left. It was still light outside; wouldn't be dark until ten. He undid another button on his shirt, muggy in here, the air a lingering mix of beer, smoke, and cheap perfume.

As he rocked back in his chair, he thought about Nash. For a second, he had a slight bout of conscience. He and Nash had been partners for years, ever since they were kids. Bowen shouldn't have taken all the money; he should have left his so-called friend with something.

Bowen shook his head, quickly changing his mind. Why should he care? Nash had his whole life in front of him; he'd plenty of time for second chances. He was sick of Nash's lectures. Nash wasn't any different. He was just better at hiding it.

To be fair, Nash was great in his day. He was probably one of the best con men around. But he'd grown soft over the years, especially after all that mess with Hilditch. It was as though he'd lost the fire inside, and all that was left was a solitary flame, waning like his reputation.

People feared Nash once. The has-beens and wannabes who now treated him with disdain had once been wary of approaching him.

Nash was still smart all right, but these days when it came to Bowen, he was too soft. He always had that weakness. Even though his philosophy was to trust no one. But why shouldn't he? Bowen was Nash's only friend, practically blood.

After the Hilditch incident, seeing the change in Nash, Bowen asked if he could manage their finances. Nash agreed without protest. 'Okay,' he said. 'I'll do it as a favour.' He often said stuff like that, an annoying habit of his, listing all the good things he'd done as though wanting you to be grateful. Bowen felt like killing him sometimes. Well, trying to at least.

Nash might not have been the man he was, but he was still smart, and he was tough, and getting rid of him wouldn't be easy. No, this was the best way. Nash would get over it soon enough. Bowen had put up with Nash for too long, and these last few weeks, every time Bowen looked at him, he'd been reminded of that kid who died up at Bron Hall.

Bowen dreamt of the kid almost every night. Nash wasn't the only one with ghosts.

Bowen took a swig of his pint. It was a stupid idea to come back. This was HolyHell all right, and once he'd finished his drink, he'd get the HolyHell out of here. Get the ferry and spend his money and his last few weeks on women and drink. He could be anonymous there. No one would go looking for him in Ireland.

. . .

AFTER SIX MORE PINTS AND three whiskies, Bowen was still
thinking about leaving. He was more relaxed. He even
bought the blonde at the bar a few drinks, which not only
encouraged her but for the last forty minutes Joanie, as she
called herself, sat next to him reeling off her life story.
Bowen hadn't listened to a word, nodding between each
pause and making the occasional eye contact to feign
interest.

Joanie was looking tidier the longer he spent with her,
and there was a willingness in her eyes as her leg brushed
against his. He was in no fit state to drive. Her place would
be as good as any, better than the car at least. His only
concern was that she'd a husband at home waiting up for
her, but he would deal with that if he had to.

Joanie stubbed out her cigarette. 'Listen to me going on
about myself; we've hardly said a word about you.'

Bowen stared at the smouldering cigarette, and the
smudge of lipstick on its filter. He hated it when people did
that. He'd gotten the habit from Nash, and as he pressed the
dog end into the ashtray, he imagined Nash saying, *why can't
people do things properly?*

Bowen looked at Joanie and smiled. Her blue eyeshadow
did her no favours. 'There's nothing interesting about me,'
he said, which, judging by the look on her face, seemed only
to intrigue her.

She pushed her fringe from her eyes and leaned closer.
'I don't believe that. Where are you from?'

'Around here.'

'Really? You sound like you're from London.'

'Moved down there twenty years ago, after I got out of
the army. I haven't been back here since.'

'Why?'

The question took him by surprise, and he almost told her the truth. Bowen nodded at the window. 'Why d'you think?'

Joanie smiled. 'I know what you mean, but I wouldn't live anywhere else.'

'Local girl through and through, huh.' He took a swig of his pint, thinking: *it's a good job because no other place would have you.*

He put his hand on her lap, relishing its warmth. She let it rest there awhile, slapping her hand down on his when he started smoothing it across her thigh. 'I'm not that kind of girl,' she said, and flashed him the diamond ring on her finger. 'I've been engaged six months now.'

Bowen tried picturing the poor fool who'd proposed to her, some council estate dope, falling in love after his first shag and declaring his devotion ever since.

'What does your fiancé do?'

Joanie beamed. 'He's a foreman in Courtauld's factory.'

'Is that place still open?'

'Yeah, they're laying off, though.'

Bowen lifted his hand off her lap and slipped it around her waist.

'Get off, I told you I'm not like that.'

Bowen looked her in the eye. 'Come on, you cock-teasing little bitch, we both know that's not true.'

Joanie stood up and threw her drink into his face. 'You cheeky fat bastard, don't you dare speak to me like that.'

Bowen wiped the splashes of gin from his eyes, then shook the collar of his shirt. It surprised him how composed he was. Normally, he'd be up like a shot, tipping over the table, his shovel-like hands gripping Joanie's throat. But the drink made him tired, numbed his senses. As he stood, he felt a stickiness between his fingers. He loathed the smell of gin; it reminded him of his mother.

He raised his hand, held it there as the voice behind him said, 'Both of you calm down now.'

Bowen looked over his shoulder and fixed his eyes on the barman. The young man looked a lot shorter on this side of the bar. He wore his flared jeans at half-mast, and his tight flannel shirt showed the sweat stains under his armpits. His hair was the biggest blow wave Bowen had seen, parted in the middle, its ash-blond highlights aging the kid before his time.

Before Bowen could answer, Joanie started shouting. 'He started it, George. You should have heard what he said.'

'Joanie, calm down,' George said.

'I will but tell this pig to apologise.'

George squared up to Bowen, opened his mouth to say something, but as he stared into Bowen's eyes, he remained silent.

Joanie placed her hands on her hips. 'Well, tell him then.'

Bowen stared at George, daring him to say something. The kid looked away, turned to Joanie and said, 'Let's just forget about it, all right.'

'No, I won't, George. I'm not frightened of him. The fat, bald pig needs to apologise. Who the hell does he think he is?'

Bowen considered whether to knock her out. Gender never mattered to him. He didn't discriminate when it came to someone mouthing off. He knew her kind. Thinking she could say what she wanted because she was a woman, badgering some dope to defend her honour and, if he was unlucky, take the hit for her.

'I'm not apologising to a whore,' Bowen said. It wasn't the smartest thing to say. But the drink got the better of him.

With her big, blue eyes bulging, Joanie lunged at him. Even this drunk, Bowen was fast, catching her hand before she could dig her long, painted nails into his skin. He gripped her wrist, leaning back as Joanie swung a punch.

Growing more frustrated, she kicked him in the shin. It hurt like hell and Bowen threw her towards the wall. She fell back onto the corner bench, the red padded leather cushioning her fall.

The whole pub was watching now, and two women ran over to her, asking if she was all right.

'No, I'm not,' she shouted through her tears. 'Call the police, look what he did to me.'

'I was trying to restrain her,' Bowen said. 'She attacked me.'

'Call the police, George,' someone shouted.

Bowen picked up his briefcase, deciding it was time to leave.

Before walking out, he slammed a fiver down onto the bar. 'Give everyone a drink on me and keep the change.' He fixed George with a stare. 'I didn't want any of this. What happened to her was an accident.'

George grabbed the fiver and put it in the till. 'Get out, or I'll call the police.'

Bowen nodded, then smiled. George suddenly found his voice, especially now Bowen was leaving.

Bowen staggered to the door, looking over his shoulder as he swung it open. 'You're all living in HolyHell, and you're gonna die in one.'

. . .

As he fumbled with his car keys, Bowen could sense everyone in the pub watching him through the windows. They were badmouthing him no doubt; barman George and his cronies probably boasting how they were about to give him a slap. He had half a mind to go back in, scare them all by grabbing a bar stool and smashing all the optics. It was something he would have done a couple of years ago. But these days it was only a thought, and the last thing he needed was the police.

Bowen opened the driver's door and slumped into the seat. He pushed the key into the ignition and started her up. The car sounded as tired as he was, as though something was rattling inside the engine. He shifted into first, released the hand brake. The car moved forward, but it didn't feel right. He pressed a little harder on the gas, changed to third, and drove a steady twenty through town.

The potholed road was in the same state of disrepair as it had been on the day he left. The pavements weren't any better, loose flagstones, the high kerbs jutting out. There must have been at least four bins positioned throughout the town. Yet dog-ends, chip bags, cans and empty crisp packets still littered the street.

The town had lots of pubs and by the time he'd parked by the Town Hall clock, he'd already counted six. All of them looked dead, amber-lit dives, hosting underage drinkers, and forgotten old men.

He glanced up at the clock and checked its time against his watch. The clock was fifteen minutes slow. What else could you expect in this place?

Bowen took a deep breath. He felt sick now, definitely in no fit state to drive along the coast. He needed to sober up, so he held the briefcase under his arm, got out of the car, locked it, and started walking.

He made his way through town, occasionally pausing when he saw something familiar, Greenhills Menswear, Hilary's Chippy, and Dirty Jack's old paper shop. He wondered if Dirty Jack was still alive and selling cigarettes to kids. He used to sell them as singles, a penny a cigarette, which was a significant margin now he thought about it.

Bowen wiped his hands down his face, sighed, then took a left up Bron Hill. Sweat seeped through his shirt, its cheap cotton chafing his skin. The soles of his feet burned, and all the weight he was carrying did him no favours. The drink tried to convince him he could walk all night, but his body said otherwise.

He stopped to take a breath, his bleary eyes gazing into the distant vermillion sky. Fire-orange clouds glowed across the hills, and the setting sun cast the trees black. Even hell could be beautiful at times.

Bowen started walking, then crossed the road and took the footpath to Bron Woods. He knew he would end up here, eventually. For weeks now, the ruins of Bron Hall pulled him like a magnet. Why kid himself? It was the only reason he came back.

THE FOOTPATH LEADING into the woods was narrower than he remembered, overgrown with nettles and weeds, each twist of ivy trying to trip him up. He and Nash spent a lot of time here when they were kids until that fatal day at least.

He could smell it now: the peaty soil, the leaves, the distinctive scent of garlic. The heat accentuated it and the baked, fetid smell of the earth triggered a thousand memories.

The path led him to a clearing in the woods. Bowen stood still, a sinking feeling in his guts. Bron Hall had hardly

changed, slightly more dilapidated, but the mock-Tudor
facade, the flaking walls, and burnt rafters made the place
haunting.

Bowen stared into the ruins, its dark shadows filling
him with dread. He glanced up at the roof, thinking it was
one hell of a drop. The oak support beams reminded him of
the kid and how eager he'd been to climb. Danny Greer was
his name. The kid was only fourteen. Hell, he and Nash
were only three years older. Greer followed them around
for weeks, pestering to join them and be a part of their
scams.

'You've got to pass the test first,' Nash said, and to this
day, he claimed he was only teasing.

'What test?' Greer asked.

Bowen intervened then. 'You need to go up to Bron Hall,
climb to the highest point on the roof, and jump off.'

They'd left it at that, thought no more about it until
someone found Danny Greer's body three weeks later.

They'd found Greer in this very spot, face down in the
rubble, with his neck broken. The police said it was probably suicide, but no one knew for sure. It shocked the entire
town; it was as though an enormous black cloud descended
over the place. Someone mentioned they saw the kid
hanging around with Bowen and Nash. Luckily, nothing
came of it, and a month later, Bowen and Nash started their
national service.

Tears welled in Bowen's eyes. He tried to shake it off,
knowing the drink was getting the better of him. *Stupid kid.
Who in their right mind would do something like that?*

He took a few steps forward, gazed up at the roof.
'Stupid kid,' he shouted. 'What the hell were you thinking?'

For years, Bowen never cared. But recently he'd started
wondering what had gone through the kid's mind, years of

subdued guilt perhaps, or a last plea for redemption before he met his maker.

What did it look like from the top? What convinced Greer he could survive the jump?

Perhaps the kid thought he had a chance. Perhaps he considered his options and hadn't blindly followed Bowen's instructions. If that was the case, it made Bowen less responsible and, in God's eyes perhaps, worthy of forgiveness. Only one way to find out and, with the drink egging him on, Bowen climbed.

BOWEN RESTED his briefcase on the ground and climbed the remains of one wall. The wall gave him just enough extra height, letting him reach one beam from the second floor and, with considerable effort, pull himself onto it. He rested his stomach on the beam, his legs dangling. He remained in this position for a few minutes, a little breathless, his thoughts caught between the ridiculousness of it all and whether he could reach the top.

He'd committed himself now, and as he shuffled across the beam, he thought, to hell with it.

His reach gave him an advantage, and he grabbed a brick jutting out from the upper wall. He pulled down on it, testing the weight. It felt secure enough, letting him press his other hand into the beam, lift one of his legs onto it, then press in with his knee and pull himself up. His arms ached. His body trembled. Every breath burned inside his chest.

His limbs felt like jelly as he stood on the second floor. Half of it was missing, although what remained looked sturdy. He took a deep breath and patted the dust off his clothes. Although his efforts only made things worse, his big hands smearing sweat and dirt across his shirt. Bowen sniffed one of his armpits. Jesus, he was stinking. He'd get down in a minute and find a hotel. But he'd climb onto the roof first and try to silence those niggling doubts.

Bowen fixed his eyes on the branches twisting through the glassless window. He stepped lightly towards them, more so when he heard the floor creak. He paused for a moment, bending his knees slightly, before pressing down on them to see if the floor would take his weight. Unconvinced it would, he stopped and gazed up at the roof and the remains of the rafters. It looked easy enough to climb, but he decided against it. He still had a good view of the surrounding woods, and for a drunken man, he was already too high up.

It was getting dark now, the last traces of light fading into the blackness of the trees. Bowen noticed the silence and a pang of loneliness flashed inside him. He never enjoyed being alone. No, that was more Nash's kind of thing.

Bowen shook his head and sighed. Those trees were too far away to break the fall. That crazy Greer just jumped, probably ruining both their chances of redemption. He didn't know whether to laugh or cry. He did neither and decided to climb down.

As Bowen stepped away from the window, he heard something, a shuffling, the snapping of dried twigs. He looked towards the trees, his heart thumping as Danny Greer's gaunt, white face stared at him through the half-darkness.

Bowen cried out, then stepped back, not looking, not thinking, and before he had time to do any of these, he tumbled to the ground.

As Bowen's head slammed against a concrete slab, he felt something in his spine snap. He tried to move, but his body was a dead weight, his limbs refusing to budge.

Voices whispered into his ear, people he hadn't spoken to or seen in years. Mostly, he heard his father's voice, but Bowen was too weak to answer.

It was as though his body was still falling.

Feelings of regret, anger, sadness, and relief rushed inside him.

His vision dimmed until all he saw was Danny Greer's ghost, the boy's sad eyes looking down at him.

Bowen tried to speak, tell the kid how sorry he was, and ask for forgiveness. Instead, he just puked over himself, his eyes rolling to the back of his head as death claimed his last breath.

PART I

POLICE AND THIEVES

1

SAD SWEET DREAMER

Jay dreaded walking past Marshall and his gang at the best of times. It was worse now, ever since his photograph appeared in the *Evening Chronicle*. 'A local boy, thirteen-year-old James Ellis, found a man's body in the Bron Woods', said the first line. Jay cut the article out and pasted it into his scrapbook. He'd read it to his mam several times, even when she stopped listening. She'd been attentive when the police questioned him, though. Full of thank-yous and smiles, acting like the best mam in the world. Even Jay almost believed it, and no one would ever have guessed she spent the last weekend drinking. It wasn't entirely her fault. Jay blamed her new boyfriend, Shane. In fact, Jay blamed Shane for most things.

Jay cast the image of Shane from his mind. Marshall and his gang were the current threat, and he needed to focus on the situation. Being bionic would help, like the guy from the TV, Steve Austin, *The Six Million Dollar Man*. Now if Jay were bionic, he could run past them at 70 mph, or hurl them twenty feet into the air. But he wasn't, so the only thing he could do was wait.

He spied on them from the landing window, peeping through the net curtains. They couldn't see him. He'd already tested that.

Things weren't so bad a few weeks ago. Marshall and his gang used to hang out near the garages. But the police kept moving them on, and now their favourite haunt was the bus stop opposite Jay's house. He sneaked out through the back door a few times, but they cottoned on to it and lately they'd been watching out for him.

Before Jay had his picture in the paper, they'd only called him names. 'What's that smell?' they'd shout. 'Hey, skunk, tell your mam you need a bath.'

Their words bothered him at first. He was just as clean as them. He had a cat's lick every morning, when he remembered. Admittedly, he'd been cleaner when his mam was with Stan. Stan washed and ironed Jay's clothes, kept the house tidy and made him have a bath every Sunday. Stan cried when Jay's mam told him she'd met someone else. He begged her not to leave him. Then Shane arrived, slapped Stan around a bit, and threw him out of the house.

Jay missed Stan a lot. But he was also angry at him for being so weak.

As Jay turned away from the window, he saw Shane coming out of the bathroom. He looked like a giant, tattoos covering his muscular arms, his tanned skin glistening against a backdrop of steam. Shane wiped his face with a towel then threw it on the floor. He flicked his hair back, parting it down the middle with his fingers. His blond mane was thinning, although nobody would dare to say that.

Shane hooked his thumbs into his jeans pockets and swaggered across the landing. Shane thought he looked cool with that stupid walk. But most of the time it made him look like a prick. Jay's mam loved it. She kept saying it was sexy, how Shane reminded her of Billy Blue Cannon from *The High Chaparral*. Jay disagreed. Shane's eyes were brown for a start, and his bushy eyebrows and big sideburns made him look kind of mean.

Shane flashed Jay a smile. 'What are you doing indoors in this weather? I've told you before. I don't want you in the house during the day. Now go outside and play.'

Jay didn't move. He liked to try his luck with Shane, see how far he could push him. He'd come close a couple of times, but Shane only clipped his ear. Lately, he kept warning Jay about his mouth, threatening to give him a hiding.

'Come on,' Shane said. 'Don't make me tell ya again.'

Jay looked Shane in the eye. 'This isn't your house, telling me what to do. You're not my dad.'

Shane laughed. 'No, I'm not, and thank God for that.'

Jay flinched as Shane stepped forward. He could smell his aftershave. The new one. Denim. *The smell of a 'real' man.* As usual, Shane used too much. Jay pulled a face. God, he could almost taste it. Shane must have read his thoughts because he grabbed Jay's arms, turned him around, and marched him downstairs. 'I'd rather smell like this than have BO. You skinny little tyke. You stink.'

When they reached the hall, Shane released one of Jay's arms and opened the front door. He shoved him outside. 'Go on, on your way.'

Jay frowned. 'Where to?'

'I don't know. But you and the fresh air need to get reacquainted.'

Jay remained standing on the path. He looked to his left, eyeing the weeds and the scorched grass. 'How's about I tidy the garden?'

Shane shook his head and with his long, bony finger pointed at the old, rusty gate.

JAY SENSED Shane watching him as he stepped onto the pavement. Marshall and his gang fell silent the moment they saw him, and before Jay ran off, they gathered around him.

It was the same old routine: Marshall calling him skunk, searching his pockets for loose change and cigarettes. Marshall and Brett were almost eighteen, five years older than Jay, and they were a few years out of school.

Jay wondered whether Marshall was pure evil. He certainly looked the part: tall, broad, with a big, square head. All he needed were two bolts in his neck and he'd look like Frankenstein's monster. Or Wanking-Stein more like, and Jay smiled as he thought of it.

Marshall mustn't have liked that because he poked Jay in the chest and asked him about the man's body and what he'd told the police. Jay went over it countless times, but Marshall kept asking him.

'You just found this guy in Bron Hall?' Marshall said.

Jay nodded.

'And what did he say to you?'

'Nowt, he was dead when I got there.' He was keeping his story consistent, just like he'd told the police.

Brett, Marshall's second-in-command, pushed his angry, sunburnt face into Jay's. 'Liar, I don't believe you.'

Jay felt his heart in his throat. 'I'm not,' he said, fearing Brett was onto him.

Brett grinned. 'Yes, you are. He wasn't dead. I bet you put your hand down his trousers first, wanked him off, then sniffed his undies.'

Marshall and his cronies burst into laughter. 'Yeah,' Marshall said, 'and just before he died, he played with your tiny cock too.'

Jay didn't say a word. He didn't like what they were saying, but he'd rather this than any of them knowing the truth. 'He was dead when I found him,' Jay said. 'Then I ran down to the phone box and called for an ambulance.'

Marshall stopped laughing. 'And you've been acting like the big man ever since.'

'No, I haven't.'

Marshall pushed his face closer, his smoky breath breezing across Jay's skin. 'Why do you look so smug in your picture, then?'

Jay never replied when Marshall was like this. He could never give him the right answer. Marshall twisted his every word. Any minute now, Jay sensed Marshall would march him down to the woods.

Last summer, Marshall shot at Jay with an air rifle and afterwards, when he caught Jay near the gorse bushes, put the lit end of a cigarette in his mouth. When Jay mentioned this to his mam, she seemed upset at first, then told him to toughen up. He knew she wouldn't speak to Marshall's parents. Like most people on the estate, she was afraid of them. Jay understood why. Marshall's parents were as crazy as their son. The only person they were wary of was Shane, but he didn't care. In fact, he encouraged it.

JAY FELT the spittle on his face as Marshall said, 'You're charged with lying. We're going to trial you down the woods, and if we find you guilty, we're going to hang you from the Curly Wurly Tree.'

Marshall meant every word. In fact, Marshall and his

gang had done it before. Jay heard stories about them hanging some rich kid, a dentist's son from the flash houses up on Wedgewood Heights. They just left him there. The kid would have died if some old guy walking his dog hadn't found him.

Jay felt his heart beat faster, as though any second now it would burst out of his chest. His body trembled as though he'd come out of a fight. He considered kicking Marshall in the shin. Then he'd make a run for it, and if they caught him, play the 'scared little kid' and start pleading. Luckily, he didn't have to do any of that because the moment Marshall saw Jay's mam on the pavement opposite, he set him free.

Marshall and his cronies stared at his mam. So did Jay. He wished she wouldn't dress like that: lace-up suede platform sandals, denim shorts, and a skin tight vest that had a picture of an American flag.

She'd dyed her hair recently because Shane said he preferred redheads.

Jay knew his mam was beautiful, but she didn't need to plaster her face with makeup. Most times, he wished she was like those mothers he saw in the high-street wearing blue trouser suits, and in the winter, beige-coloured macs. He mentioned this to her once, and she laughed, then said, 'Sorry, love, you're stuck with me I'm afraid. What you see is what you get.'

She nodded slightly, beckoning him closer. As Jay walked towards her, he paused and glanced over his shoulder, giving Marshall a defiant look. He knew Marshall wouldn't do anything. Not because he feared Jay's mam, but because he was frightened, it might get back to Shane.

When Jay turned to face his mam, she grabbed his arm and started walking him up Moor Hill. She stopped about a quarter of the way up, then in a hushed voice said, 'You keep away from them.'

'I tried to,' Jay said, 'but Shane kicked me out of the house.'

'I told you not to go winding him up.'

Jay frowned. 'I didn't; he started on me.'

His mam didn't answer. Instead, she mumbled something to herself, then glanced over her shoulder as though distracted by something. Jay sighed a few times to get her attention, and when she did finally look at him, she said, 'What were you talking to them about, anyway?'

'That fella I found in Bron Hall, what I told the police, they're always asking.'

'You need to ignore them then, don't you.'

'I can't, Mam. They're always watching out for me. They grab me every time I leave the house.'

She shook her head and smiled. 'Don't you worry; I'll tell Shane to have a word with them.'

Jay nodded, at least Shane was good for something.

As though reading his mind, his mam gave him a harsh look. 'But don't you do anything to encourage them.'

Jay clenched his fists and looked down at the pavement. How come it was always his fault? He never did a thing.

He fixed his eyes on the white plastic carrier bag she was holding. She'd been down to the offy again, bought a few bottles of wine and a load of cans. That only meant one thing, she and Shane were going to spend the entire day drinking.

No wonder the big-headed bastard wanted him out of the house. Jay didn't mind his mam being drunk so much. She just acted stupid and got over-emotional. But Shane grew nastier with every sip.

Jay's mam slipped her free hand into her pocket and

pulled out a crumpled pound note. 'Here, go on, take it. Get yourself something from Woolies and make sure you buy some chips with the change.'

Jay forced a smile. He was desperate not to appear ungrateful; a quid would have been a fortune a few weeks ago, but not now.

His mam studied him for a moment, then sighed. 'Do you have any mates from school you can play with?'

Jay shrugged.

'No one at all?'

He shook his head, although it wasn't entirely true. He had a few mates, but he didn't know their addresses. Most of them lived in those new houses, or near the school; he was the only kid in his class from the Moor Estate.

His mam reached out her hand and pushed her fingers through his hair. 'You'll have to get this cut before you go back to school.'

'But I like it long.'

She laughed. 'Yeah, me too. It suits you.' She turned towards their house, then looked over her shoulder and said, 'You keep safe, huh. Don't stay out too late or go wandering into town; I don't want you too far from the house.'

Jay nodded, watching her for a second before turning around and sprinting towards the top of the hill.

HE WAS A SUMMER CHILD, or so his mam kept telling him. It was the reason he loved the sun, the heat, and every golden splash of light. It hadn't rained for months now, but that still didn't stop people from complaining. Especially the old folks who kept moaning it was too hot.

Jay loved the muggy nights and those warm summer

breezes. He loved going around with his shirt off or walking barefoot on the hot tarmac roads. This was his best summer ever, especially after what happened these last two weeks. He wished it would never end, but like all the good things in his life, he sensed it would. It didn't bother him too much. He'd be leaving soon, and he was more worried about that. In a few weeks, he and his mam would start a new life.

When he reached the top of the hill, he stopped, and looked across the Greenfield Valley towards the estuary. He hadn't been there for a while. Until the stranger's death, he'd been spending his time in Bron Woods and neglected the estuary for weeks. He longed to return there now. The tide was out, revealing stretches of golden sand. From where he stood, the water didn't look so wide, a ten-minute walk at the most, but he knew it was wider, five miles at least, or so Stan told him. Jay always wanted to find out for himself. He planned to walk across to the other side one day. But that would have to wait now. Something to do when he came back, years later, when he was older.

The thought of leaving this place saddened him. Then he felt nervous, wondering how he was going to persuade his mam. She'd see sense, though. He knew it. The only problem was getting her away from Shane. There was no answer to that right now, and he cast such thoughts aside, turning his back on the estate, and started walking to town.

When he was a quarter of a mile down the road, he heard music blaring from someone's window. He recognised the tune immediately, *Our Kid's* 'You Just Might See Me Cry'. One of his favourites. His mam bought him the record, but Shane banned him from playing it in the house, stopped him singing it too. Shane reckoned Jay sounded like a cat drowning or someone in extreme pain. Jay knew it wasn't true. He had a great voice. Loads of people said so. He'd prove Shane wrong when he was famous, wipe the smile off his face by appearing on *Top of the Pops*.

Singing always made him feel good. He never felt embarrassed. He'd sing anywhere, loud sometimes, even when he was walking down the street. He would change the words as well, or build a story around it and imagine he was the star of the film. He did that now, leaving all his troubles behind him; then he stopped, his heart in his throat as he caught sight of Bron Woods.

Lately, he dreaded seeing the place. Not so much because of the man who died there, but it made him feel guilty, then the worry crept in, took root, made him anxious and filled his head with all kinds of scenarios. What if the police found out he'd been lying, or worse still, discovered the truth? Jay shook his head. Nah, he was being stupid. He never meant to frighten the man. What the hell was he doing up on the roof, anyway? That money was his now, finders keepers, losers weepers, that was the rule in these streets.

2

THE BOYS ARE BACK IN TOWN

Nash guessed something was up weeks ago. Bowen was surlier than usual, distant, and contradicting everything he said. Nash tried to make a joke of it at first and asked him if it was his time of the month. Bowen didn't like that. It made him worse, so Nash thought his best line of defence was to ignore him.

Two weeks later and Bowen still hadn't been down to the Bull's Head. Nash didn't pay it much heed, assumed his old friend was still sulking. He guessed Bowen had gone on a bender to Brighton or somewhere similar. He'd be back soon enough, hung over, his thick bushy tail between his legs.

Nash felt envious. At least Bowen was enjoying himself, which was more than could be said for him. For weeks now, Nash spent these hot, sticky Saturday afternoons indoors, watching *World of Sport* with a bunch of no-hopers in this smoke-filled, dimly lit bar. To make things worse, Pete the Chink sat next to him. He reeked of BO and his deeply tanned skin matched the colour of the table.

Pete wasn't even Chinese but to look at him you'd swear

he was, especially when he smiled. Nash never liked it when Pete was smiling, because usually it was linked to someone's misfortune. But what he hated most was how Pete had been overly familiar. Years ago, Pete wouldn't have dared to even look at Nash the wrong way, let alone speak to him. Pete called him *Mr. Nash* back then, hanging onto his every word, as humble as Uriah Heep.

These days, this short, nicotine-stained, emaciated-looking man was as disrespectful as the rest of them.

Pete slapped a folded newspaper on the table. 'You heard the news, Nash? It's in all the headlines.'

Nash shook his head. His eyes fixed on the TV as he stubbed out his cigarette. He remained quiet, trying not to encourage Pete.

Pete stared at him for a moment. 'Aren't you going to ask what?'

Nash sighed. 'Come on, enlighten me.'

Pete unfolded the paper and pointed at one headline. 'Bowen's dead. They found his body a few weeks ago.'

Nash felt a lump in his throat. 'What the hell are you talking about are you drunk or something?'

Pete grinned. 'No, I'm not.' He tapped his finger on the paper. 'See for yourself. It's there in black and white.'

Nash grabbed the newspaper and gave it a shake. He turned to the front page. 'This isn't the *Standard*.' It was the *Evening Chronicle*, the paper from where he grew up.

Pete nodded. 'I know, Bernie Sideburns gave it to me.'

'What the hell's he doing with it?'

'He was up there last week, has a sister near there.'

Nash didn't answer. Instead, he scoured the headlines still refusing to believe it. 'What the hell are you rambling on about, Pete? I can't see anything.'

Pete snatched the paper from Nash's hand and flicked through a couple of pages. 'Here, look, on page eight.'

Nash spread the paper out on the table. MAN FALLS TO HIS DEATH AFTER CLIMBING SIDE OF BUILDING. *George Royston Bowen, forty-one years old.* How they knew Bowen's full name and age, he hadn't a clue. They must have found his driving licence or something. *Royston*, even in these circumstances, the name still tickled him. Nash scolded himself and carried on reading.

The article didn't say much. It just mentioned the old Bron Hall, and there was a picture of the boy who found him. The kid reminded Nash of himself when he was that age.

After reading the article a few times, Nash pushed the newspaper aside. He closed his eyes and let out a deep breath, more from shock than grief. He couldn't get his head around it. Bowen hadn't been back home for years. Trying to climb Bron Hall, what the hell was he thinking? He repeated the questions in his mind until a foul smell reminded him who he was sitting next to.

Pete's eyes shone with contentment. A look perfected from years of gloating over other men's misfortune. Nash considered giving him a slap, gripping Pete's grimy shirt collar, and hoisting him off his seat. But all he did was look away. He had more important things to think about.

'Are you all right, Nash?' Pete said. 'You look a little upset.'

Nash stared at him. 'What do you think?'

'I believe you are. I would be if it were me.'

'But I'm not you, am I, and I thank God every day for that.'

Pete frowned. 'There's no need to be like that. I was only

saying. I know you're upset, but there's no reason to be nasty.'

The way Nash felt now, nastiness was his only option. Pete was testing him, pushing, and pushing, and it took all his resolve to stop himself from grabbing Pete's greasy hair and slamming his face down on the table.

Nash subdued his anger. Words and intelligence were more his kind of thing. So why change the habit of a lifetime? Instead, he took out a cigarette, popped it in his mouth, then gestured to Pete for a light.

Nash took a deep drag, blew the smoke into Pete's face, knowing it would annoy the hell out of him.

Pete waved the smoke away with his hand. 'Poor old Bowen, huh, so what are you going to do about it?'

'What do you mean?'

Pete wiped the moisture from his lips. 'Well, there's the funeral to attend, although you've probably missed that. Then there's his flat to sort out, and, if I know Bowen, there'll be money involved. You'll have to sort out his finances.'

Nash didn't respond. As usual, he remained expressionless. He would not give this scrawny piece of dirt a thing. Within himself, however, the story was entirely different. His heart thumped inside his chest like an alkie knocking on a brewery's door. His head was all over the place and he tensed his muscles to stop himself from shaking. He was shocked to hear about his old friend, but all he could think about was the money. He'd always been like that. Any sniff of trouble and his survival instincts kicked in.

As Pete rambled on, Nash thought about the bank. It was the weekend. The place wouldn't be open until Monday. The realisation of this was like a kick in the teeth. He could hardly contain himself now, never mind making it through Sunday. He could always drink himself stupid and forget about it for a bit, but knew that wasn't really an option.

He fixed his eyes on Pete and gave him one of his sad looks. 'I can't think about finances at a time like this, Pete. I've been friends with Bowen for years, ever since we were kids.'

'It's rocked you a bit, huh?'

Nash nodded with an expression of exaggerated dismay, sensing Pete was enjoying every second.

Pete slipped his hand into his pocket and took out a crumpled roll-up. It looked as though it had been festering inside his pocket for weeks. It turned Nash's stomach to watch the tip of Pete's tongue slither along the paper's edge, and he almost retched at the string of saliva attached to it.

Pete popped the cigarette into his mouth, struck a match, and held the flame to its tip, drawing on it for a while before he got the thing to light. He took a deep drag, then blew out a thin wisp of smoke, which, for the effort he'd made, barely seemed worth it. He flicked the ash onto the carpet then looked at Nash. 'I can help if you like? It's a lot for you to take in. I'm more than happy to go to Bowen's flat, sort things out.'

'What things?'

'You know, lecky, gas... the bank and stuff.'

Nash nodded. 'That's very kind of you, Pete. Why would you want to do that?'

Pete flashed him a crooked smile. 'That's what friends are for. I just want to help.'

Years ago, such blatant insincerity would have angered Nash. He would have seen it as an insult to his intelligence. Did they honestly think that since all that mess with Hilditch he'd lost his ability to see through bullshit? Did they actually believe that these days he was taken in by a few kind words and a fake smile?

It made Nash laugh to see how many people gave themselves away. The slight hint in the eyes, their body language, told him everything he needed to know. No, he hadn't lost the gift. He'd perfected it, and as the years went by, the more he embraced it. He was happy to let them assume he was over the hill. It gave him so many advantages. People's arrogance, selfishness, and greed allowed him to play them for the fools they were. Human frailty was a wonderful thing.

Nash kept that in mind as he stared into Pete's shark eyes. 'That's very kind of you, Pete. But it's a lot to ask of someone. I'm sure you've got enough problems of your own.'

'It's not a *problem*. I'd be more than happy to help.'

Nash toyed with him for a second. 'I don't know.' He studied the glimmer of hope in Pete's eyes. 'No. No, it's too much to ask.'

'But—'

'No, Pete, I wouldn't dream of it. You've already done your bit. Thanks for the offer, though. But you've got enough on your plate so let's say no more about it.'

He stood and nodded at Pete. 'I'll be seeing you then,' he said, relishing Pete's frustration as he made his way to the door.

SUNDAY HAD BEEN a hell of a day, but not in the way Nash expected. He'd gone to Bowen's Flat, but the landlord was out. Three hours he waited, drinking warm tea in the café across the street. He ran out of patience in the end, nothing to show for his time but a swollen bladder and a stomach full of eggs and bacon.

Nash spent the rest of the day and most of the evening looking for his chequebook. Not that he used it that much; his line of work, when he could get it, was paid in cash, and these days, his only dealings with the bank was when Bowen nudged him for his monthly payment.

He'd been giving Bowen money every month for years, and they'd saved quite a tidy sum. Nash tried to keep on top of it at first, checking their account regularly, reviewing the statements. But after that mess with Hilditch he lost interest. Bowen was straight when it came to money. He was the only person Nash could trust.

Even now, Nash knew their money was safe. His only concern was how to get his hands on it. But that was almost sorted now. He'd found the account number and on a scorching Monday morning, sat in the manager's office of the MidWest Bank, he was minutes away from a fortune.

Mr. Tattum was an officious type, beaked nose and turtle-necked, his greasy, straight hair looking as though a bowl had been used to shape it. He wore a grey, pin-striped suit and thick, National Health glasses. This surprised Nash a bit because, on a bank manager's salary, surely Tattum could afford to dress more stylish. His deep voice didn't match his appearance. Nash wondered if the girls in the bank had a nickname for their boss. Something like Tattum Turtleneck or Touchy Tattum if he couldn't keep his hands to himself.

When Nash told Tattum about Bowen's recent demise, he looked at him stony-faced. Nash expected him to say something, but Tattum didn't, not even a 'Sorry to hear that.'

He continued to act like this throughout the entire conversation, occasionally nodding whenever Nash asked him a question. The only time he showed a modicum of

emotion was when Nash informed him he wished to withdraw all funds and close the account.

'Very well, Mr. Nash,' he said. 'Just bear with me for a
moment.'

NASH CHECKED HIS WATCH. Tattum had been gone for over
fifteen minutes. What the hell was the man up to? For what
felt like the hundredth time, Nash glanced around the room.
He couldn't work in a place like this. Too confined, not
enough light getting through the small window. The big oak
desk was nice enough, and the green leather chair looked
eloquent. But that was about it. The atmosphere was stifling.
It was a poky little hole with hospital-blue walls and metal-
grey filing cabinets. Nash shook his head and sighed. Hell, a
man could lose his soul here.

Finally, and much to Nash's relief, Tattum walked into
the room. He held a large brown file and looked agitated.

Tattum sat down behind his desk and slowly opened the
file. He stared down at it for a second. 'Are you sure you
want to withdraw the funds and then close the account, Mr.
Nash?'

'Of course. Why? Is there a problem?'

Tattum removed his glasses and rubbed his eyes. 'Not
really. It's just that...'

What the hell was this turtle-necked prick talking
about? He forced a smile.

Tattum put his glasses back on, that officious look of his
instantly returning. 'Well, are you aware that you only have
one pound fifty in your account?'

'*One pound fifty*, what the hell are you talking about?'

Tattum plucked a sheet of paper out of the file. 'See for
yourself.' He pointed at a column of numbers.

Nash scanned the statement. 'These are all withdrawals. . . Jesus, we'd saved over fifty thousand.' He studied it closer. 'The bastard! Sorry, Mr Tattum, please excuse my language.' He paused for a second. 'According to this, Bowen was drawing money out of the account every month.' He fixed Tattum with a stare. 'You authorised this?'

Tattum shifted in his chair. 'Yes, I did. Why shouldn't I? It was a legitimate request.'

'But I signed nothing.' Nash regretted saying that as soon as the words left his mouth. Not only was it reactionary, but it was a stupid thing to say.

Tattum breathed deeply. 'It's a joint account, Mr. Nash. You and Mr. Bowen signed the mandate when you opened it, giving each of you the right to deposits, withdrawals, to sign cheques.'

Tattum put his hands together as though readying himself for prayer. 'I can imagine all this has come as a bit of a shock, especially with the recent news concerning Mr. Bowen. All I can advise is that you contact the authorities.'

Nash nodded, 'Hmm, the authorities.'

'Yes, the police, your solicitor. As you're probably aware, you may have a legal claim to those funds.'

Nash stared at him. Authorities. People in his line of work didn't go to the *authorities*. 'Thanks for the advice, Mr. Tattum. I'll see what I can do.'

Tattum's face softened and there was the hint of a smile. He handed Nash a sheet of paper. 'Give this to one of the girls at the counter and they'll give you the remaining funds and close the account for you.'

With the sheet of paper in his hand, Nash stood up. 'Thank you again for your time, Mr. Tattum. It's very much appreciated.'

Tattum followed him to the door. 'That's not a problem,

Mr. Nash. My door's always open. I'm just sorry I couldn't have been more help to you.'

Like hell you are, Nash thought, smiling as he shook Tattum's hand.

NASH FOUND nothing of value in Bowen's flat, so after fifteen years of hard work and savings, all he had to show for it was a dead, lying scumbag of a friend and one-pound-bloody-fifty. He didn't know whether to laugh or cry. Sooner or later, he would probably do both. It was a good thing he was driving. Kept him focused. It wasn't just the money, or so he told himself. No. It was the principle of the whole thing.

His grandfather's words bounced inside his head: *Always remember, son: trust no one.*

Nash followed that advice all his life with only one exception. He felt stupid. It was an awful feeling. A fool was something he'd always gone out of his way not to be. But who could blame him? He'd known Bowen nearly all his life. They grew up together, known each other since they were two snot-nosed kids. When it came to money, Bowen never put a foot wrong.

Nash felt more gutted the more he thought about it. He had money stashed away but only for a rainy day, nothing to see him through a storm. The strange thing was, he hadn't thought about it until now. He plodded along like the rest of them, head in the sand, getting through each day. He should have paid more attention, asked to see statements, split the money into different accounts. He should have done a lot of things. But he hadn't. The only thing he had done was realise that hindsight was a wonderful thing.

He shook his head, sighing as he pressed lightly on the brakes. The traffic was slowing now, and in a few minutes would probably come to a stop. He'd been lucky, to be fair. The M1 was almost a straight run. Now he hit a bottleneck, everyone heading north and piling onto the M6.

When his car came to a stop, Nash turned on the radio. He flicked through the stations until he found something he liked, *Thin Lizzy's* 'The Boys are Back in Town'. This was more like it, much better than those red-faced, cider-drinking hicks singing about their bloody combine harvester.

As he shifted in his seat, Nash felt the sweat trickling down his back. He leaned forward, his shirt sticking to him like a second skin. There was no end to this heat, not that he was complaining. The TR6 convertible gave him a slight advantage in this weather. It was better than being baked alive like these poor souls in front of him. Bowen never approved of Nash's TR6. He said it was too flash. Men like them needed to be inconspicuous. A man shouldn't draw attention to himself. That might have been true in northeast Wales, Nash thought, but in London, nobody cared.

Anyhow, his TR6 wasn't new, and underneath the bonnet, it was probably on its last legs. All these stops and starts didn't help; this model overheated, and that was the last thing he needed.

THE DRIVE UP from London to the A55 took him just over six hours. The sign at the border read *Croeso i Gymru - Welcome to Wales*. Nash didn't sense any welcome. He felt the opposite in fact, and as he drove through the small border towns, his heart filled with dread.

The towns had changed little in all these years. Granted they had a few new supermarkets, and someone built a block of flats. Other than that, the endless rows of red brick houses, the factories, the steelworks, and the glimpses of the estuary between them looked no different. They even smelled the same: a mix of sea, sand, petrol, and baking dust.

The sun melted into the horizon leaving a soft, orange glow in its wake. For as long he could remember, Nash loved this kind of light. It made the place seem dreamlike, that halfway point between light and darkness as the evening turns into night.

As Nash reached the Well Hill, he saw the graffitied sign welcoming him to *HolyHell*. Bowen probably saw it too, and Nash smiled to himself as he imagined how his friend reacted, with loathing, probably, another thing to trigger his temper.

Bowen never bought into nostalgia. He hated this place more than Nash. But not enough to stop him from coming back.

Nash sighed at the enormity of his task. What led him here? Was it the gut feeling of a seasoned pro, or a frightened man's last hope? There were so many unanswered questions. But Nash was tired and sweaty, and they were questions he couldn't face right now, questions that would have to wait until the morning.

As Nash turned right towards the fire station, he caught sight of a B&B. He didn't remember it being there before. It was a big blue house next to the old convent. He took a sharp left into the driveway. There was plenty of parking space, and except for a pale-yellow Reliant Robin, his was the only car there.

Nash grabbed his book and got out of the car. He had brought nothing else. He left London in a rush when all he could think about was how to get his money back. As he knocked on the front door, he realized how ill prepared he was. He didn't have a change of clothes. Hell, he didn't even have a toothbrush. Perhaps the B&B would help him out. If not, he'd get something from town in the morning.

The man who answered the door was a sour-looking old goat. He was slightly hunched and the grimace on his grey-whiskered face seemed permanent. What remained of his hair was ruffled into white, matted spikes, and the bags under his eyes were trying to tell his body that it desperately needed sleep. The old man said nothing at first; he stood there looking angry, his small, grey eyes scanning Nash from head to toe. 'Well,' the old man said, 'what do you want?'

Nash suppressed a smile. 'This is a B&B, right?'

The old man nodded. 'That's what those big letters say, isn't it? Unless someone has stolen the sign.'

Nash fixed him with a stare. 'Then I'd like a room, please.'

The old man shook his head. 'Why the hell didn't you say so, standing there like an idiot. I thought you were one of those Jehovah Witnesses.'

Nash didn't answer and followed the old man inside. Electric fans of various sizes were placed throughout the reception area and the hall. The constant buzzing sounded like a swarm of flies trapped inside his head, although he welcomed the breeze. He hoped his room would be as cool as this; it was impossible to sleep in this heat.

Resting his weight on the makeshift wooden counter, the old man opened a drawer and took out a red notebook. He flicked through a few pages, then removed a small Biro from behind his ear. 'Name?' he said, without looking up.

'Nash.'

'First name.'

'Mr.'

The old man paused for a second, then scribbled something on the page. He looked up. '*Mr.* Nash, huh? Well, you can call me *Mr.* Jameson.'

Moody Jameson, Nash thought, but didn't say a thing.

Jameson closed his notebook and put the Biro back behind his ear. 'It's two pounds fifty a day including breakfast, and you know what you can do if you don't like it.'

Nash nodded. 'Can you do me a discount? I might stay for over a week.'

Jameson's eyelids flickered. 'Call it fourteen quid. That's the best I can do, but I don't serve a cooked breakfast on Sundays.'

With dexterous ease, Nash slipped the money from his wallet and placed it on the counter.

Jameson snatched one note and held it to the light. 'Got to be careful with forgeries.' He turned his back on Nash for a second and grabbed a key from the wall. He turned around and smiled. 'I'll give you number seven. It's the double at the back, looks out across the estuary. That okay with you?'

'Not really, I'd prefer something at the front of the house.'

The old man shrugged. 'Okay, suit yourself.' He grabbed another key off the wall. 'You can have number four. It has a *lovely* view of the main road. It's a little smaller, though.'

'Sounds perfect, I don't suppose you could sell me some toothpaste, Brylcreem, a few toiletries?'

Jameson frowned. 'No. I don't suppose I can. Does this place look like a chemist to you?'

'No, I just thought—'

'Well, you thought wrong then, didn't you.' Jameson mumbled something then walked towards the stairs. 'If you want to know where your room is, then you best come with me.'

Nash shook his head and followed Jameson upstairs.

The heat on the landing was stifling. The room was the same, the open windows making little difference. Nash put his book in his pocket, took his jacket off and slung it over his shoulder. He wiped the sweat from his face with his free hand, tasting the muggy air with every breath.

Jameson chuckled to himself. 'Boiling, isn't it. We're going to have summers like this for a thousand years, or so they say.'

'Is that right, and who are *they*?'

Jameson unlocked number four and Nash followed him into the room. 'The experts,' Jameson said. 'Those in the know. The people who write the papers. I tell ya, the world is on its last legs.'

Nash placed his jacket on the back of the chair, then glanced through the window. 'What makes you say that?'

Jameson handed him the key. 'Look around you: a plague of ladybirds, trees dying everywhere, Labour squabbling among themselves, and putting Old-King-bloody-log in Number Ten. I tell ya, *Mr. Nash*, this country has gone to the dogs.'

Nash nodded with fake interest, not quite believing what he was hearing. 'I think we'll be safe for a few years yet, Mr. Jameson. It'll probably rain in a few weeks.'

Jameson shrugged, unconvinced, then pointed at another door. 'Bathroom's through there, but there won't be any hot water until eight, if hot water is what you want. I'd keep the window closed tonight if I were you, unless you don't mind the midges all over you.' He paused on his way out and looked over his shoulder. 'I've got a small bar in the lounge. Cheaper than the pub, give us a shout later if you fancy a few cold ones.'

'I'll keep that in mind,' Nash said, sighing with relief as Jameson closed the door.

JAMESON, whose name had temporarily been upgraded to Mad Jameson, was right. All you could see from the window was the road, the houses opposite, and the fields beyond them. He was right about the heat and as predicted, the room was swarming with midges.

Nash must have fallen asleep the moment he lay on the bed because when he glanced at his watch it was almost ten p.m. He stretched, rubbed the sleep from his eyes and took in the room. God, this place was cheap. It smelled bad too. Nash reckoned the heavily scathed wardrobe was probably bought in the nineteen thirties. The ceiling was mottled with damp patches and the cheap, floral wallpaper was nicotine-yellow.

Nash lit a cigarette and shook his head at the dubious stains on the carpet. Wondering if the place could get any worse, he looked out of the window, catching the last glimpses of a dying sun melt into the distant fields.

He hadn't been back here for almost fifteen years, not since his granddad's funeral. The old man spent most of his life down the estuary, cockling in that old, battered boat. As a kid, Nash used to help him, washing things down and gathering up the nets.

It felt so long ago. Almost as though it never happened.

Nash sat up. He was wide awake now, the voice in his head urging him to go out and start sniffing around for answers. But he stayed put. His head throbbed like crazy. He was tired, and it was too late to venture into town. Instead, he took a few deep drags of his cigarette, then flicked it out of the window.

The room was looking less appealing the longer he sat there. With that in mind, he walked to the bathroom and stood at the sink. He turned on the tap, rinsed his face with cold water, then dried his hands with the manky towel.

Nash stared at himself in the mirror. He kept his hair short, side-parted with tapered back and sides. It was more a fifties look, but that's how he'd always liked it. Long hair and big sideburns just didn't appeal. It wasn't everyone's cup of tea, but he'd grown to like his face. Even his nose. Eventually.

Most days he felt handsome, but sometimes he felt like the ugliest man in the world. Certain women just didn't like him. They'd be quite vocal about it too. He'd be minding his own business, when he'd sense some woman, usually his age or younger, scowling at him from across the street. In his younger years, it really bothered him. Then his heart hardened with age, and, like most of life's disappointments, he got used to it.

The odd thing was it wasn't without its contradictions. Nash had his share of female attention. It used to confuse the hell out of him. Sometimes, he'd be walking around thinking the world was bleak, then he'd catch some woman's eye and a couple of drinks later, she would be all over him. That's how he met his last girlfriend, Red Suzy. Her hair was ginger to be fair, but she insisted people describe her as 'strawberry blonde', eventually settling for red.

Suzy claimed Nash was the most handsome man she'd ever met. Nash accused her of being deluded. But he accepted her compliments in the end because, for the brief time they were together, she believed it. That was almost two years ago, and he'd seen no one since.

He smiled at himself. It wasn't such a terrible face and, either way, he was stuck with it.

NASH GRABBED his book and went downstairs, hoping Jameson hadn't changed his mind about that drink. He found the old man loitering in the hall and by the looks of him, he'd been waiting there all evening.

Jameson flashed him a toothless smile. 'I thought you'd come down. You seem like a man who enjoys a cold one.' He placed his hand over his mouth for a second. 'Sorry, got my teeth out, giving them a soak.'

'What do you have?' Nash said, eager to change the subject.

'A few bitters, pale ales. Since the drought I've been drinking lager. I've got quite a few cans of Skol.'

'Got any pilsner?'

'Nah, too expensive, it gives you a bad head and a bad arse, too.'

Jameson went quiet for a second. 'Two cans for nineteen pence.'

'Nineteen pence?'

'I'm not a charity you know, cost you twenty-six pence in the pub.'

'Go on then,' Nash said and followed him into the public lounge.

From what Nash had seen, this room was the brightest in the house. He put it down to the large bay windows, which, in the day, let in more light, and even now after sunset, the streetlight shone through.

The room was cheerier too. Well, at least until Jameson spoiled it with his hunched shadow.

Nash sat down on the large, leather couch. It was soft

but comfortable, and modern for Jameson's tastes. The old man's wife probably bought it and Nash searched the walls, shelves, and cabinet for any family photographs. He didn't find any, and except for a few women's magazines lying on the coffee table there was no sign of the lady of the house.

'Do you run this place on your own,' Nash said, 'or is there is a Mrs. Jameson?'

Jameson pulled a face. 'Sadly, there is. But she's in Fishguard at the moment, staying at her sister's.'

The old man tapped his fingers on the bar. 'You should be thankful she's away.'

'Why?'

'She doesn't allow the bar to be open this late.'

Jameson seemed proud of his makeshift bar. You could tell that just by looking at him. There was a shine in his eyes, and he was almost another person. He opened a can of Skol and poured it slowly into a glass. 'We call this the *family* room. What do you think?'

Nash dreaded to think what type of families would spend their time here, so he just smiled, trying to remain polite. He could sense the old man watching him as he pretended to browse through his book. When he looked up, Jameson was standing in front of him.

The old man put the glass on the table and nodded at Nash's book. 'What are you reading?'

Nash closed the book. '*Meetings with Remarkable Men,* by George Gurdjieff.'

Jameson smiled. '*Remarkable men*, huh? Hmm, you'll be hard pressed to meet any of those in this town.' He glanced at the book. 'What is it, a thriller?'

'Biography...philosophy.'

Jameson grimaced. 'I can't be doing with any of that nonsense. The world has enough of that.'

Nash took a sip of beer, relishing the cold liquid sliding down his throat. He drank until he'd emptied the glass then wiped his mouth with the back of his hand.

Jameson refilled Nash's glass. 'Does the trick, huh? It's just the ticket when the weather's like this.'

Jameson was right; the lager was what Nash needed. He sat quietly, growing more uncomfortable the longer Jameson stared at him.

'You know, your face looks familiar,' Jameson said. 'Where do I know you from?'

Nash shrugged. 'I'm not sure you do.'

'Where you from?'

'Down South.'

'You grew up there?'

Nash looked over his shoulder and glanced out of the window. 'Nah, I grew up around here.'

Jameson's eyes widened. 'Is that so... Nash. Hmm, the only Nash I knew was Brynley Nash. Little fella, cockler, used to work down the old docks.'

Nash took a long swig of his drink. 'My granddad. He practically brought me up.'

'What about your parents?'

'Died, in a car accident.'

Jameson nodded. 'Yeah, I think I remember something about that.' He smiled to himself. 'He was a bad piss-head your granddad. He liked to bet on the horses as well.'

Nash finished his drink and slammed it down on the table. 'Yeah, he liked a drink, but he was a hard worker too.'

'He died in that old house of his, didn't he?'

Nash nodded then stood up.

'Yeah, that's right,' Jameson said. 'It's all coming back to me now. It was a week before anyone found him.' Jameson shook his head and sighed. 'Sad state of affairs. That's a bad way to go, dying alone like that.'

Nash glanced down at the carpet. 'I was in the army. Not a lot I could do about it.'

'But you knew he was ill, right?'

Nash stared into Jameson's eyes. 'What's with all the questions? What has any of this got to do with you?'

'Okay, keep your hair on. I was just asking.'

'Well, I'd prefer it if you didn't.'

IT WAS past midnight and Nash still hadn't fallen asleep. He felt washed out. Recent events and the long drive up to Wales took their toll. He hoped the beer would help, but it only made him drowsy and now he'd passed beyond sleep. His thoughts wandered. One minute he was stressing over Bowen and worrying how he was going to get his money back. Then he'd think about his granddad, little Bryn.

Being back here didn't help. As he watched the road from his window, he felt the valley's presence and, more so, the estuary beyond it.

In his mind's eye, Nash saw the tide rising and the lights flickering across the distant shore. The scene triggered so many memories, filled him with that boyhood loneliness. For a moment, it was almost as though he'd never left.

He pictured his granddad sitting in his boat, pot-bellied and bald, a cigarette clamped between his lips while his weathered hands fixed one of the nets. The old man was always smoking a cigarette. He'd drag on it without ever taking it from his mouth, smoking it down to the stub.

'I like to get my money's worth,' he used to say. Then cough his guts up before lighting another.

Nash started smoking aged ten. It never bothered the old

man. Most things never bothered his granddad. He was happy as long as he could work all day and stay in the pub most of the night. To his credit, he always put food on the table and if Nash ever wanted anything, he never needed to ask twice. But that was the limit of the old man's affections and he encouraged Nash to keep his distance, preferred it when he did his own thing.

'Never be too soft,' the old man always said. 'Most people see kindness as a weakness. You take care of *yourself*; trust me it's the only way.'

Years later, when Nash heard that the old man was in a bad way, he never went to see him. It was difficult. He was in the army. Those bastards wouldn't have given him leave even if he'd tried. The old man wouldn't have wanted to see him. He'd taught Nash to take care of number one.

Nash had nothing to be ashamed of. He'd been trying to convince himself of that ever since.

THE NEXT MORNING as Nash sat in the dining room, Jameson kept reminding him how grateful he should be for his breakfast.

'You won't get a fry-up as good as this for miles,' Jameson said. 'Not at this price.'

Nash stared into his plate, at the heap of cold beans, the tinned tomatoes, the burnt sausages, the fatty, undercooked bacon, and the grease-soaked fried bread.

'Yeah,' Nash said. 'It's definitely something.'

Jameson beamed. 'Too right, you get that down you and you won't eat for a week.'

'Yeah, I can believe that.'

All he could manage was a mouthful of beans. He couldn't stomach the rest and settled for the coffee instead, figuring it would keep him going until noon. As he gazed out the window, he sensed Jameson staring at him. Nash turned his head towards him.

'Problem?' Jameson said.

'No. Why do you ask?'

'You hardly ate a thing. Is there something wrong with your food? I've been up since seven cooking that.'

Nash forced a smile. 'Nothing's wrong with the food. It's just me. I'm feeling a bit anxious.'

Jameson pulled out a chair and sat opposite him. 'Oh, aye, anxious about what exactly?'

Nash put his coffee down. 'It's sensitive, but you seem like a person a man can trust.'

Nash suppressed his smile as he watched Jameson's eyes widen. He earned long ago that if you want to get a man like Jameson to help you, then tell him what he wants to hear.

'Of course,' Jameson said. 'Your secrets are safe with me.'

Nash nodded. 'I'm acting for a friend. She got some bad news a few days ago.'

Jameson's face softened, but there was a twinkle in his eyes as though the news of someone else's misfortune pleased him. 'What news?'

'A man called George Bowen. He died here a few weeks ago. You probably know about it?'

'No, I can't say I do. What happened to him?'

'Fell off the ruins of Bron Hall, tragic accident.'

'Oh, that bloody id—' Jameson stopped himself. 'Yes, it's very sad, I read about it in the papers. You a friend of his?'

'I knew him vaguely. I remember him when we were kids, but I hadn't seen him in years. His girlfriend, she's really cut up about it, wants me to see if he left anything behind, you know, for a keepsake.'

Jameson nodded with exaggerated solemnity. 'I heard they buried him in Rosehill Cemetery, welfare funeral.'

Nash released a genuine sigh of dismay. 'Who were the undertakers?'

Jameson shrugged. 'Dunno, but you've only got a choice of two. Benson's just off the high street, head to the bus station and you'll see it. Opposite Kwiks.' Jameson grabbed a cup and poured himself a coffee. 'The other one is Lloyd Griffiths on the corner of Bron Park Road, near the lights.'

'Thanks,' Nash said. 'That's been a great help to me.' He scraped back his chair and stood up. 'I better crack on, I guess. There's no point putting these things off.'

Jameson nodded. 'Give me a shout when you get back. Let me know how you got on.'

'Will do.'

Just before Nash reached the door, he paused and turned round. 'It was a kid that found him, right? I saw his picture in the paper.'

Jameson necked down his coffee then stood up. 'Yeah, a boy called Jay Ellis.'

'You know him?'

'No, but I know the family. His mother's a right little slut. Nobody knows who the father is.'

'I take it you don't like them?'

'No, I don't. I don't like most people from the Moor Estate. Scrounging bastards.'

Nash pretended to agree. 'Yeah, I know what you mean. Give them an inch and they'll take a mile.'

'Too right. You can't blame the kid. It's in his blood. Sad truth is, he'll end up as useless as the rest of them.'

'Probably, but he did a good thing, and I'd like to thank him for that.'

Jameson shrugged. 'The mother's called Renee Ellis. I

don't know which house it is. Just go to the Moor Estate, I'm sure someone will tell you.'

'I don't suppose you still have a copy of the newspaper with the article about Mr. Bowen's death?'

Jameson sighed. 'Why would I? As I told you yesterday, this isn't a chemist's, and neither is it a public library.'

NASH CALLED at the library first, seeing as it was on his way. It was stifling in there even with the doors open. The librarian's friendliness took him by surprise. She was a small, rotund woman with a tight greying perm and a penchant for smiling. The tourist board should have paid her commission because if she greeted every stranger like that, they might mistake the town for being a nice place. Nash didn't, though. No, he knew everything there was to know about this place.

The librarian showed him where they kept the old newspapers and Nash flicked through a pile of *Evening Chronicles* until he found the required dates. Then he sat down and spread a couple of weeks' worth of papers across the table. He read the original article and one follow up he found a few times in case they revealed something new or something he might have missed. They didn't. They made him feel worse, in fact, reminding him of the extent of Bowen's treachery, and how he'd lost everything.

Nash breathed deeply, much to the annoyance of the old man sitting at the table opposite. By way of an apology, he threw the old man a smile. Then he looked down at the paper and studied the picture of the boy.

On first impression, the kid looked happy enough, wide-eyed with a big smile on his face. The longer Nash considered it, the kid's smile grew less convincing. Nash could spot a liar in a crowded room. He knew when someone was faking. He guessed the kid must have been nervous, probably wasn't used to all the attention. Nash tore out the page, folded it in half, and slipped it into his pocket. Then he stood up, winked at the old man, and went outside.

He made his way to Griffiths' funeral directors first, seeing as he was already on the Bron Park Road.

The day grew muggier, the warm air forcing him to slow his pace. This weather wouldn't last forever; good things never did. These kinds of summers reminded him of when he was a boy, cloudless blue skies, and those never-ending light nights. They made him think of his granddad too, and as Nash looked across his shoulder, staring beyond the houses and the valley trees, he saw the estuary.

The tide was out, revealing a vast golden stretch of sand. That wide-open space always unsettled him. The tide could rise so quickly, catch a man unawares and reveal how fragile life was. But that wasn't the only reason he kept his distance. He always felt guilty when he went there. Then the sadness crept in, taking root. No, he stayed clear of that place, too many ghosts.

GRIFFITHS' Funeral Parlour was closed. Nash knocked at the door for at least ten minutes, but no one was in. If there was somebody there, they sure as hell didn't want to answer.

Nash headed to town, veering left before he reached the high street and cutting through the main bus station. It proved to be quite a task. A double decker had broken down and three other buses were queuing behind it. The bus inspector wasn't handling it well. He was trying to get the end bus to reverse out, but it was stuck. It was blocked from the front too, and the gap behind was too narrow. The driver's bad attitude didn't help, neither did the growing frustration of those waiting.

The inspector's fat, red face made Nash think of Bowen. In this kind of situation, Bowen would have gone ballistic. It only took a tiny spark to fuse his temper at the best of times, and as Nash slipped through the crowd and turned the corner, he wondered whether Bowen's anger led him to his death. Only God knew that and all he left behind were an empty bank balance and a heap of questions.

Nash hoped to find some answers to those questions at Benson's Funeral Parlour. The first thing that struck him when he walked in was the smell of furniture polish. It was so strong he could taste it. The shop, if you could call it that, was almost bare. He expected more than a couple of flower-less vases and an unattended counter.

He pressed the bell, its high-pitched chime making the place feel strange. The sound of someone clomping down the stairs was followed by a tall, skinny man who now stood behind the counter. He certainly looked the part, gaunt and pale, and even when he smiled, there was a sombre look on his face.

The man's small, eyes fixed on Nash. 'Hello, can I help you?'

Nash flashed him a sad smile. 'Unfortunately, yes.'

The man nodded. 'A recent loss, is it?'

'Kind of.'

'Friend or family?'

'Friend.'

The man reached under the counter and took out a black ledger. He placed it down carefully, opened it, then said, 'The earliest we can do is next Tuesday.'

'Ah, I'm not here to book a funeral. I'm here to enquire

about one. A friend of mine. George Bowen. They buried him a few weeks ago.'

The man nodded. 'Yes, we did the funeral.' He breathed deeply. 'Sad state of affairs, you know, when you're buried alone like that.'

'I know, but I only heard the news earlier this week.'

'So, Mr...'

'Nash.'

'How can I help you?'

Nash stepped forward and rested his hands on the counter. The man looked paler this close, and Nash couldn't stop staring at the grey twists of hair up his nose. 'The thing is, Mr. Benson—'

'Call me Dafydd. We like the personal touch here. I let such formalities pass away with my late father.'

Nash smiled. 'The thing is, Dafydd, I'm here on behalf of someone else. A lady by the name of Rosie Hayes; she was Mr. Bowen's partner.'

'And what does Ms. Hayes require?'

'A keepsake, something to remind her of him.'

'Hmm, you'll need to speak to his next of kin for that.'

'I didn't know he had any.'

'Yes, his first cousin. Mrs. Rollit from Pentre Halkyn. They traced her quite quickly. We couldn't have buried him otherwise.'

'Do you have her address?'

'I'm not allowed to give you that. But as I said, she lives in Pentre Halkyn. It's only a small village, Mr. Nash.' Dafydd studied him for a moment. 'I don't think she'll be very welcoming.'

'Why?'

'She has had a few nasty surprises lately, a dead cousin and now a funeral to pay for.'

'Didn't he have anything to cover it? Money? Cash in the bank?'

Dafydd shook his head. 'Not to my knowledge. He had his car, his watch, his wallet held a couple of fivers.'

'Nothing else?'

'No, not that I'm aware of.'

Nash's heart was pounding, but he composed himself. 'She has to fork out?'

Dafydd sighed. 'That's the idea. I rarely bill until two months later, so hopefully her solicitors will have sorted out the estate by then. Perhaps he's got a house somewhere, something she could sell. But he was a friend of yours, right?'

'To be honest with you, not really. I only met him a few times, but I'm here on behalf of his partner.'

Dafydd took a deep breath. 'Well, I hope you find her something. It's a tragic state of affairs. Such a stupid way to die, but I suppose the cancer would have got him, eventually.'

'Cancer?'

Dafydd lowered his voice. 'Lung cancer, quite advanced. They told me that at the hospital. They have a tendency to talk, you know.'

Nash nodded in agreement. 'People usually do.' He covered his mouth for a second, trying to hide his surprise. 'I heard it was a kid that found him?'

'A local boy. He was playing in Bron Hall. Mr. Bowen's body might have been there for days if he hadn't found him.'

He fixed on Dafydd and through a forced smile said, 'Thanks for everything. You've been extremely helpful.'

'Not a problem, Mr. Nash, and good luck finding that keepsake.'

· · ·

WHEN NASH WAS A BOY, what was now the Moor Estate was mostly fields, rolling hills, and farmland that receded into the wider valley and broke off onto the estuary. Now it had a crop of cream-coloured terraced houses and a steep, tarmacked road that branched out into lanes and avenues. There were only a few cars parked on the estate, a rust-worn Cortina, an old Austin 1100, and an orange Ford Capri. There were plenty of dogs, though, mongrels mostly, either mooching around dustbins or lazing against garden gates.

Most houses had the windows and doors open. Music blared out onto the avenues, the Wurzels telling the world about their *brand-new combine harvester*. Nash whistled the tune as he walked down Moor Hill, knowing it would stay in his head all day. These types of songs stuck to you like a bad memory.

He stopped halfway down the hill, hoping to see someone. There was no one in sight. The only hint of life was the faint sound of kids playing in the distance. He headed towards it, quickening his pace when he saw the playing fields. As he was about to cross the road, a bus turned the corner. It stopped in front of him, and two women and a man got out. Nash smiled at them, but only the woman holding the shopping bags smiled back.

'Excuse me,' he said, raising his voice slightly as the bus rattled past.

The woman's smile wavered. 'Yeah?'

'I was wondering if you could help me? I got a call out, concerning a power outage. A Mrs. Ellis, but they didn't give me her full address.'

The woman stopped smiling. 'You've just passed it.' She pointed to the house opposite the bus stop. 'Number twenty-two.' Then nodded her head as if to say *leave me alone now and don't ask me another thing.*

Nash took the hint and thanked her with a smile. He turned round and headed towards the house, stopping when he reached the gate. The garden was tidier than he expected, although, it still hadn't been touched for a while. The flowers were wilting, the grass getting longer, just a few days away from that shabby look of neglect.

He opened the gate, walked up the garden path and knocked on the front door, lightly at first, tapping harder when no one answered. He peered through the letterbox, but all he had was a limited view of the hall. The house was part of a terrace, so there was no access to the back. Nash sighed and turned around in defeat.

Before he reached the gate, he heard something and glanced over his shoulder at the house, fixing his eyes on the boy watching him through the open upstairs window.

Nash turned to face him and smiled, but the boy just stared at him. 'Are your parents home?'

The boy shook his head. 'No, Mam's in town. She won't be back for ages.'

Nash nodded, wiped the sweat from his brow, then fanned himself with his hand. 'That's okay. It's you I came to see.'

As the boy's expression changed from sulky indifference to a look of shock and fright, Nash lit a cigarette. He took a deep drag, exhaling a stream of smoke as he said, 'Don't look so worried. There's no need to be afraid. I'm here to thank you.'

The boy pushed his head out further. 'Thank me, for what?'

'You're James Ellis, right?'

The boy nodded. 'They call me Jay.'

'Thank you for doing the right thing and trying to help a friend of a friend. You're a local hero.'

The boy blushed. 'All that stuff happened weeks ago.'

Nash flicked the ash from his cigarette. 'I know, but I'd still like to speak with you.'

The boy studied him for a moment. 'You'll have to wait until my mam gets back. She told me never to speak to strangers.'

Nash nodded. 'That's sound advice.' He forced another smile, catching the worried look in the kid's eyes as the boy slammed the window shut.

3

THE WANDERER

Peeping through a gap in the net curtains, Jay watched the stranger for almost an hour. Time dragged, and at one point he thought the man would never leave. It was a relief when he did but the panic which swelled inside him finally took its toll. Bile burned in Jay's throat, his legs weakened, and, for a moment, he struggled to catch his breath.

He sat down on the edge of his mam's bed and closed his eyes for a second, trying to calm himself.

The stranger knew. Jay was sure of it.

He couldn't explain why, he just sensed it. It was something he'd been able to do ever since he could remember. People gave so much away. Not so much by what they said but by the little things they did. With the stranger it was his smile, and there was something in the eyes, too.

Jay took a deep breath then stood up. Only one thing to do, he needed to hide the money in a safer place.

· · ·

JAY TOOK the long route to the spot, in case someone
followed him. He wore his football shorts and the red
Manchester United vest his mam bought him. He wasn't a
big United fan, but he liked Stuart Pearson's hair. He bought
the single they'd released too, mainly for the B-side because
it mentioned the *Six Million Dollar Man*.

Jay dreamed of being bionic and had the money to do it
now. The thought took hold of him as he walked across the
fields. He jogged, slowly, exaggerating each movement as
though he was running in slow motion. Occasionally he'd
jump over a dried-cowpat or a tuft of dead grass. He made a
noise when he did this, trying to mimic the synthesized
sounds that Steve Austin made when he ran. Jay could never
make it sound as it did on the TV, but he came close. He
kept this up until he reached the valley woods, his mind
wandering as he sauntered through the trees.

The hot afternoon air stank, a fuse of mud, dead plants,
and wild garlic. Jay's head throbbed. He felt sweaty, his
sunburnt skin smarting. Shafts of sunlight fell through the
gaps in the trees and in the distance, splashes of gold
reflected across the Flour Mill Pool, the Flouy as they
called it.

Jay raised his right arm and sniffed his armpit, regretting
that he hadn't used Shane's deodorant before he left the
house. He'd go to the swimming baths later and stand under
the shower for ages.

He could have been anywhere wandering among those
trees, the Black Forest, even the Canadian Rockies fighting
the Sasquatch. His mind drifted there, but only for a
moment. The high-pitched screams and laughter quickly
reminded him where he was.

Jay remained hidden in the woods. There would be
loads of kids at the Flouy, teenagers mostly, sitting on the

pool wall, smoking cigarettes and listening to their transistor radios. The older boys wore cut-off jeans instead of shorts, impressing their girlfriends by bomb-diving off the wooden walkway. Even Jay had to admit it was cool, and some of the older boys looked cool too. Jay tried to copy their hairstyles, growing his hair long, shoulder length and parted down the middle. He wore a gold chain around his neck, the one Stan gave him before he left. He'd repay Stan's kindness one day and, with that in mind, he quickened his pace, focusing on his task.

He followed the path through the woods, kicking up the dried mud, snapping the brittle twigs. He picked up a dead branch and lobbed it down the bank, watching it tumble into the ferns. When he looked towards the path, he saw something from the corner of his eye: a dog, a crow, or probably just a shadow. Whatever it was, it kept still, and Jay sensed it watching him. Then he saw it again, creeping through the long grass. He jogged, moving faster as he heard something behind him. He didn't dare to turn around. Fear urged him on, as did the advancing sound of his pursuer's breath and the heaviness of its tread. Jay sensed there were others too. He could hear their whispers and the sound of muffled laughter. As he was about to break into a sprint, two big, clammy hands gripped his shoulders. Jay tried to pull free, but it was no use. They were too strong for him.

'Get off me,' he shouted. Then he fell silent as one of those clammy hands covered his mouth. The other yanked his hair, pulling him backwards. The scorched earth felt like concrete, and a sharp pain shot through Jay's back. The assailant sat on Jay's chest, pressed his knees into Jay's arms, pinning him to the ground.

Jay stared into Brett's angry face.

Brett grinned. 'We've got you now, you little bastard.'

He pushed his face closer, his hot breath stinking of cigarettes. 'Think you're clever, don't you? You cocky little prick. We've got something big planned for you.'

MARSHALL and his gang took Jay to the top of the woods, forcing him to climb over the barbed wire fence that ran parallel to the path. Then they marched him through the long grass until they reached the old oaks.

The *Curly Wurly Tree* was the tallest and the easiest to climb. Jay had reached the top lots of times and had carved his initials into the bark. He felt no fondness for the tree today. Its thick, leathery bark and sweeping branches filled him with dread. He felt his heart inside his throat and the weakness in his knees almost forced his legs to buckle under him. But he kept standing, mostly through fear.

All of Marshall's gang turned out for the main event. They gathered around Jay, waiting expectantly while Asprey, the runt of the litter, went to fetch a rope. To kill time, Marshall reminded Jay of the charges against him. Not that there would be a trial. No, Jay was already guilty.

'Bullshitting's the main crime,' Marshall said. 'Then there's your bad attitude, and being a stinky, poncey little prick.'

Tears welled in Jay's eyes but for now, at least, he held them back. He struggled to get his words out. 'Just you wait till Shane hears about this,' but his voice sounded sluggish and thick.

Marshall laughed. 'Shane doesn't care about you. I bet ya if I ask him, he'll help us.'

Jay remained silent, knowing it was probably true.

He considered trying to buy his way out but thought

better of it. Once Marshall knew about the money, it would be the end of everything: his hopes, his dreams, him and his mam's fresh start. He tried to call Marshall's bluff, pretending he didn't care.

'You're not going to do anything,' he said. 'You're the one full of shit.'

Marshall stared at Jay for a second then slapped his face. 'Show some respect. Don't ever speak to me like that again.'

Jay couldn't decide what was worse, the humiliation, the pain, or the tears streaming down his cheeks. He'd let himself down. He felt pathetic and weak. Anger swelled inside him as Marshall's cronies pointed and laughed.

The afternoon heat was unrelenting, and a low sun cast long shadows. He wanted his mam. But he'd settle for any adult. He shut his eyes, wishing for someone to stroll by and ask Marshall and his gang what they were doing. When he heard a rustling in the grass, he opened his eyes, hoping his wish had come true.

The sight of Asprey's round, freckled face sickened him, as did the thick, oily rope slung over Asprey's shoulder. Asprey looked eager to please, and there was a swagger in his step, as though he was a knight errant returning victorious. He offered Marshall the rope, the light in his eyes fading as Marshall snatched it from his hands.

'Took your time, Aspirin,' Marshall said and turned his back on him.

As though he'd been doing it for years, Marshall quickly made a noose, slipped it over Jay's neck, then slung the other end of the rope over one of the top branches. Then he nodded at Asprey and ordered him to climb to the top.

Asprey dragged his heels at first but when Marshall threw him one of his looks, he soon hurried up. He shifted up the tree like a mountain goat, coiling the rope around the branch until Marshall was satisfied. Asprey was all fingers and thumbs, struggling to tie the knot. When he finally did, he let out a sigh of relief, his joy short lived because Marshall told him to stay put.

Fear sped the beat of Jay's heart. Marshall was actually going through with this. Jay's only option was to escape and as futile as it seemed, he was going to try. He lifted the noose from his neck and made a run for it, but Brett and Marshall were too quick, and Jay only managed a couple of feet before Brett blocked his way and Marshall grabbed his hand.

Marshall pulled Jay towards him. 'Come here, you little bastard. You're going nowhere.'

He gripped Jay's arms, holding them firm while Brett slipped the noose over Jay's neck.

'Help me carry him up,' Marshall said. 'Then we'll let him swing.'

Brett nodded. 'You sure the rope's short enough?'

Marshall grinned. 'Yeah, I reckon there'll be a few feet between him and the ground, enough to see him squirm, see him do a little dance.'

He threw Jay over his shoulder as he would an old rag and carried him up the tree. Brett followed, grabbing Jay's ankles and wrists whenever he tried to break free.

As a last act of defiance, Jay bit Marshall's shoulder. It had little effect. Marshall just gave a faint yelp and rammed the heel of his hand into the side of Jay's head. It knocked Jay sick, and for a short while, all he heard was a ringing in his ears. By the time he composed himself, they were already halfway up.

Marshall lowered Jay off his shoulder, leaned him against the tree, then ordered him to stand up.

Jay's legs trembled as he balanced himself on a branch.

He tried not to look down, but he couldn't help it. They must have climbed at least eight feet. If the rope didn't kill him, the fall certainly would.

Marshall tightened the noose around Jay's neck. He lowered Jay down in stages, stopping now and then so that Brett could take Jay's weight.

For Jay, it played out like a dream, a strange nightmare from which he'd never awake. Time slowed. All he could hear was the thick beat of his heart as the smell of soil and sweat flooded his senses.

The rope burned across his throat and tightened as his legs rested on Brett's shoulders.

All Brett had to do was step forward, and Jay would suffocate to his death. Such a pathetic way to die. He shouted for his mam, longed for the soft, loving grace of her touch.

'Look, he's gone and pissed himself,' someone shouted, and Jay cried as the wet warmth settled around his crotch.

As Brett's shoulders slipped away from him, Jay struggled to breathe. He gripped the rope with both hands, tried to pull himself up. It was no use. He kicked at the air, the surrounding laughter and his sense of panic intensifying.

Even though Jay's eyes were open, the light drew away from him. The boys' voices faded, sounding off into the distance. Jay had no more strength, the pain swelling in his chest as he succumbed to the darkness. A high-pitched sound passed through him like a knife. Death had claimed him, and he felt his body rising.

WARM AIR BLASTED into Jay's lungs. Someone pressed down on his chest. He reached out, his vision blurred, trying to move their hands away.

'Are you alright, bud?' said the figure leaning over him.

It was a man's voice. He recognised it from somewhere. Jay tried to answer but couldn't get his words out. He nodded, gulped in some more air, then mumbled, 'Where's my mam?'

'Don't know, bud,' the man said. 'Do you want me to fetch her for you?'

Before Jay could answer someone said, 'She's pissed out of her head probably, getting shagged by Shane.'

Then Jay heard laughter, and everything came flooding back.

Jay tried to push himself up, but his body was too weak. His head thumped and as he turned onto his side, he almost puked. His vision was clearer now. As the man helped him sit up, Jay recognised him immediately. He was the man who called at his house a few hours ago.

The man's smile made him look different. Friendlier. It was a kind face. The kindest face Jay had seen in ages.

'You rest for a while,' the man said. 'Then we'll get you home.'

Jay nodded. He watched as the man stood up and turned to face Marshall.

'What the hell was all that about?' the man said.

Marshall shrugged. 'We were just having a laugh.'

'You've got a sick sense of humour then if you get your kicks hanging a kid from a tree.' The man wiped the sweat from his brow. 'You'll get twenty years for this.'

'For what?'

The man glanced at Jay, then fixed his eyes on Marshall. 'Attempted murder.'

'*Murder*?' Marshall said. 'We weren't going to murder him. He only swung for a few seconds. We were just about to lift him up before you poked your nose in.'

The man took a step closer. 'And how do I know that?'

Marshall flashed him a defiant smile. 'Because I say so, and you should believe it if you know what's good for you.'

The man stared at Marshall for a second. 'How old are you?'

Marshall appeared taken aback by the man's question. He threw Brett a glance. 'Almost eighteen. Why?'

The man nodded. 'Old enough then.'

'Old enough for what?'

The man answered by punching Marshall in the stomach and knocking him down. Marshall lay on his back, winded, his eyes watering. The man glanced down at him and smiled. 'You'll live as soon as you catch your breath.' He turned to face the rest of the gang. 'Luckily, for you lads, I'm not going to call the police. But you better scarper before I change my mind.' He pointed over his shoulder at Marshall, 'And take that gobshite with you.'

Marshall's gang didn't need telling twice. Brett and Asprey helped Marshall up, walking him towards the valley as the others trailed behind. The man stood and watched, motioning for them to keep walking whenever one of them looked back. The moment the gang was out of sight, the man walked over to Jay and rested on his haunches. 'How are you feeling?'

'All right,' Jay said.

The man narrowed his eyes. 'Are you sure? You look a bit pale to me.'

Jay nodded and motioned to get up, but the dampness around his crotch kept him grounded. He breathed deeply, blushing as he pulled his vest down to hide the wet patch.

The man flashed him a sad smile. 'Don't worry about that, bud. It'll soon dry off.'

He stood and offered Jay his hand. 'The name's Nash. Come on, let's get you home.'

THEY WALKED IN SILENCE, the sun beating down on them as the smell of dried grass and baking mud hung in the air. Wary birds watched them from the trees, shafts of golden light cast long shadows. In the distance, Jay could hear kids shouting and jumping into the pool. A girl's high-pitched scream resonated through the trees, then faded, followed by the sound of laughter and a dog barking.

They kept to the path, their breath heavy, occasionally exchanging glances. Nash didn't look modern, Jay thought. In fact, with his short hairstyle and pale blue suit, he looked like someone from the 1960s, one of those tough guys from the American movies. He looked cool. No one could deny that.

'All right?' Nash said.

Jay blushed, realising he'd been staring. He pushed the hair from his eyes, nodded, then said, 'There's no need to walk me home, you know. I'll be okay.'

Nash patted Jay's shoulder. 'Yes, there is. I need to know you're safe.' He stopped for a moment to take out his pack of cigarettes. He popped one into his mouth, took out his lighter, and flipped open the lid.

Holding the flame to the cigarette's tip, Nash drew on it until it was lit. He snapped the lighter shut, took another drag, and released the smoke through a sigh.

'What's the score with that gang? Why have they got it in for you?'

Jay shrugged. 'They just don't like me I guess.'

Nash nodded. 'Seems to be the case. Some people just

like to hate. They don't need a reason.' He fixed his eyes on Jay. 'You know all that stuff they tell you about bullies?'

'Yeah, that they're cowards and you should stand up to them.'

Nash smiled. 'Yeah, that's about it. It's right sometimes, but not always. Some bullies are just mean, afraid of no one.'

'Marshall's like that.'

'You mean the big, ugly one who gave me lip?'

Jay laughed. 'Yeah, that's him.'

Nash took a quick drag of his cigarette. 'I could tell that just by looking at him, saw it in his eyes. Only ever stand up to that kind of bully when you're sure you're going to win the fight.'

'And you reckon that would stop him?'

Nash continued along the path with Jay walking alongside him. 'It would make him think, that's for sure. Especially if you hurt him.'

'It might just make him worse.'

'Might do,' Nash said. 'But that's the chance you've got to take.'

The path was suddenly cut short by an old wooden gate. Jay climbed over it, waiting on the other side while Nash unfastened the rope and swung it open.

'Blasted thing,' Nash said. 'Who on earth tied that?'

Jay didn't answer. He carried on walking, slowing his pace until Nash caught up.

'I'd never take that chance,' Jay said. 'Marshall will always be stronger than me.'

Nash took a drag of his cigarette. 'I'm not too sure about that. Lots of things change with time. But even if that was the case, there are still so many kinds of fights. There're lots of ways to hurt him.'

'Like what?'

'I don't know. Something that will cause him grief, sting him enough so he'll always think twice.' Nash pointed at his head. 'The thing is, bud, a man needs to use his loaf. He has to think his way in and out of things, use his brain to improve the situation.'

Jay kind of understood but wanted an example. Yet any questions he might have had were silenced as the path led them onto the estate. It was the strangest feeling and as he took in the rows of cream-coloured houses, the unkempt gardens, the blaring music, kids shouting, and the blackened windows reflecting the sunlight, he was overcome by a sudden feeling of dread.

For the last half hour, he'd travelled from a nightmare into a dream. Death almost claimed him. But he'd defied it, taken the path through the trees, walked alongside his saviour. That's who he thought Nash to be, although he'd never have the courage to tell him that.

The Moor Estate was a reality check, as was the hot tarmac road cutting through it. Bin bags lined the street. The rancid smell of rotten food, like an omen, warning the world of the pestilence to come. It seemed only Jay took heed. Even Nash who, Jay assumed, was probably the smartest person he'd ever met, appeared oblivious to the impending danger.

Perhaps it was all in Jay's mind. He was too sensitive. His mam was always telling him that. The most trivial things would upset him. A change in the weather, someone's tone, the look on a stranger's face. Maybe it was the aftershock or the realisation that his time with Nash was almost over. His walk with Nash reminded him of the times he'd spent with Stan, and as he caught sight of his house, he realised the Moor Estate always made him feel sad, robbed him of those brief moments of joy, and, if he ever allowed it to, would gladly rob him of everything else.

As they approached the house, Jay tried to persuade Nash not to follow. 'I'll be all right now. I can walk the rest of the way myself.'

Nash was not listening or hadn't heard him. He didn't say a thing. He just kept walking, holding his smile as he opened Jay's front gate.

Jay walked ahead, then turned, quickly, shutting the gate in front of him.

'See you around,' he said, standing firm while Nash tried to push it open.

Nash frowned. 'What's wrong?'

'Nothing, I just need to go in, that's all.'

As Nash was about to answer, someone opened the front door. Jay looked over his shoulder and saw his mam, her arms folded, standing on the top step.

'You all right, love?'

Jay turned towards her. 'Yeah, I'm brill, just on my way in.'

Jay waited for his mam's smile, but she looked angry. She fixed her eyes on Nash, frowned, then said, 'Can I help you?'

Her voice sounded slurry. It always did when she'd been drinking.

Nash pushed open the gate and walked halfway up the path. He rested his hand on Jay's shoulder. 'Your son had some trouble down the woods. A gang of boys tried to hang him from a tree. I don't know if they were messing around, but either way it could have had grave consequences.'

Jay's mam went red in the face. She glared at Jay. 'I've warned you haven't I, told you to keep away from them.'

'It wasn't the boy's fault,' Nash said. 'Those lads were hounding him.'

Jay's mam nodded towards the door. 'Come on, Jay, get inside. I'll speak with that Marshall in the morning.'

Jay motioned towards her, stopping when Nash said, 'We can see him now if you like?'

Jay's mam stepped forward, 'And how is this any of your business?'

Nash smiled. 'Like I said, I helped your son in the woods. They hung him from a bloody tree. He passed out. If I hadn't been there, God knows what might have happened to him.'

'And you are?'

'Nash.'

'Well, *Nash*, thanks for your help, but I'll sort it out myself, if that's all right with you?'

She grabbed Jay's arm and hurried him into the house, then slammed the door in Nash's face.

Jay followed his mam into the front room. 'Why do you always have to be so rude? What did you do that for?'

She turned to face him and, screaming at the top of her voice, said, 'I told you to keep away from them. I bloody warned you. You stay away, or I swear to God I'll hang you myself, I will, I'll bloody marmalise ya.'

'It wasn't my fault, Mam. They followed me down the woods.'

'Why didn't you run off then?'

'I tried to.'

'You're staying in from now on. I don't need this, Jay. Keep away from that Marshall and don't bring any more strangers to this house. I don't want people poking their nose into my business. I've enough to worry about.'

Jay pointed at the red mark around his neck. 'Look, look what they tried to do to me.'

She stared at him. Tears welled in her eyes.

He stretched his neck. 'See. What are you going to do about it?'

'Don't raise your voice at me, and I'll have less of your cheek.'

'I'm not being cheeky. I asked you what you were going to do about it.'

'I'm warning you, Jay, watch your mouth.'

'No, I won't.'

She raised her hand, tried to clip his ear, but Jay was too quick for her. She tried again but Jay kept dodging her, and she grew more frustrated at every failed attempt.

'Get to your room,' she screamed.

He turned his back on her, stormed into the hall and ran upstairs. He grabbed the fiver he'd hidden under his mattress and came back down.

'Get back up the stairs,' his mam shouted from the front room.

'No,' Jay said.

'Get up there now, Jay. Don't make me wake up Shane.'

He opened the front door and went outside. He could hear her shouting at him as he hurried down the path.

'Get back here now,' she screamed. 'I'm warning you.'

'Warn me all you like,' he mumbled and slammed the gate behind him.

Jay hated her when she was like this, screaming and shouting, every time she was upset. Why couldn't she be like other mams, throw her arms around him, ask if he was all right? He knew it was mostly the drink. She'd regret it later, sobbing and hugging him, telling him how sorry she was. It still didn't make it right, and he often wondered who was the grown-up.

He kept the fiver clenched in his fist as he walked up

Moor Hill. 'Fat cow,' he mumbled. 'Bloody fat cow.' He felt bad saying it. His mam was all right most of the time, and she certainly wasn't fat. He took a deep breath, the tears almost getting the better of him. He quickened his pace, breaking into a jog when he saw Nash walking down Station Road.

'Hey,' Jay shouted. 'Hey.'

Nash turned around, and Jay ran towards him.

'How's it going, bud?' Nash said. 'Everything all right?'

Jay nodded. He opened his mouth to say something, but no words came out. Instead, he offered the fiver to Nash.

Nash stared at it for a second. 'Why are you giving me this, bud?'

'To say thanks.' Jay felt himself blush. 'For helping me before.'

Nash glanced down at Jay then stared at the fiver. 'That's a lot of money to be giving away. Where did you get that from?'

Jay paused for a second, his heart thumping as he considered telling Nash the truth. 'It's from my mam. She told me to give it to you.'

Nash stared into Jay's eyes. 'Now that surprises me. When we spoke just now, she seemed furious.'

'She always gets like that, especially when she's upset.'

Nash nodded. 'Fair enough, but I don't want a reward. Don't get me wrong, I don't mean to be ungrateful.' He placed a finger across his lips, then rested it on his chin. 'I best come back with you and say thanks to your mam. I—'

'No, you... you can't do that.'

'I'm sorry?'

'It'll embarrass her, start her off again.'

'But I need to thank her.'

'No, you don't, please, promise me you won't mention it to her.'

Nash held out his hands, palms up. 'Okay, simmer down. I won't say a thing.'

'Swear to it.'

Nash let out a laugh and with a grave expression on his face said, 'Cross my heart and hope to die.'

Jay smiled, shoved the fiver into Nash's hand, then ran off.

PART II

NOW IS THE TIME

1

HELP YOURSELF

Nash paid no attention to old man Jameson rabbiting on, he was too busy wondering what to do. Young Jay definitely had his money. The kid probably found it next to Bowen's body, and the only question now was how to get it back.

Nash couldn't just go storming in. Threatening the kid was too risky. It wasn't Nash's style, especially after all that mess with Hilditch. He could see how brave Jay was. The kid would not give up his treasure so easily. The boy had passed his biggest test when those idiots tried hanging him from a tree. Nash couldn't help but like him, but still needed to take back what was his.

He needed to befriend the boy somehow. But at the moment, Jay's mother stood in the way. Nash only needed a few minutes with her to know what she was all about: gobby and in your face. There was no point trying to charm her; he wasn't her type. She probably went through men as quickly as a glutton in a pie shop. The bullshitting type, he guessed. Younger, tall, and good-looking, tattooed, reeling off their lies to anyone foolish enough to believe them. He'd probably have to be a bit handy, too. Nash smiled to himself. She'd find plenty of those in this town. One or two in every pub.

Nash looked at Jameson and sighed. The old codger cornered him the moment he got in, nosing into how he got on, and pestering to join him for a drink.

'First one's on the house,' he said. 'I'll even drop my prices.'

It was funny how friendly people became when you confided in them and boosted their ego with compliments. Jameson wouldn't shut up, rabbiting on as though they were best mates.

The old man complained mostly, jumping from one subject to another, the heat, Callaghan's government, and now he sounded off about the trial of armed robber Donald Neilson, aka, The Black Panther.

Jameson didn't seem interested in the four dead people. He focused more on how clever Neilson was and didn't show any remorse for the man's victims. Nash guessed the old man would probably feel different if he saw the bodies close up. He'd seen grown men puke at the sight of blood. Jameson would be no exception.

Jameson shook his head and laughed, slammed his newspaper down on the table and prodded it with a long, bony finger. 'You've got to give it to this Neilson. He gave the coppers a right run around.'

Nash didn't answer. He'd read about it in the papers and hadn't been impressed.

'He used to form patterns of behaviour,' Jameson said. 'It says here he'd steal a radio and chuck it a few hundred feet away from the house. Then when the coppers cottoned onto it, he'd start doing something else. The idiots never linked a thing.'

Nash nodded and smiled, almost tempted to inform the old man that there was nothing impressive about that. It was one of the oldest tricks in the book. Neilson was an amateur, deranged. He changed his name from Nappey; who the hell wouldn't? He must have taken some stick about that, no wonder he turned into a psycho. Admittedly, he pulled off some good jobs, but he got sloppy, greedy, hoodwinked by fame.

That's what distinguished the professional from the amateur. Pros knew how to weigh the odds. A pro understood his limitations and Nash learned that the hard way.

Nash had been involved in a couple of sloppy robberies when he first left the army and soon discovered it wasn't his thing. He thought too much for a start, which put him at odds with his colleagues. Adrenalin junkies mostly, less interested in the money and more motivated by the rush.

No, Nash never fitted in, and probably would have had a hard time of it if he hadn't been able to handle himself. His granddad was to thank for that. The old man taught him how to fight, taught him that sometimes things could only be settled by violence. Nash hated admitting to it but in his world that was true, even though he did his best to avoid it.

These last few years, Nash and Bowen were *details* men, reconnaissance, research, finding that Achilles heel, those who couldn't be found, buying and selling information. They made a lot of money from it too until Bowen went AWOL.

Nash smiled to himself. Yeah, pros knew their limitations all right, and no amount of planning ever guaranteed success. You always had to keep one thing in mind, life is random, and Nash knew all about that.

He took a swig of beer and sighed, feeling a bit bloated.

He stretched out his arms. 'That's me done I'm afraid, gonna head up to bed.'

Jameson pulled a face. 'It's not even ten o'clock.'

'It's been a long day, traipsing here there and everywhere. I need to rest.'

Jameson grinned. 'That's why you need a drink. Anyhow, you still haven't got what you came for.'

Nash froze for a second. 'What do you mean?'

'Your keepsake. You said you were going to visit your friend's cousin.'

'That's right, so I did.'

Jameson stood, walked over to the bar, and grabbed two more cans of Skol. 'That's why you need another drink.'

Nash rubbed the tiredness from his eyes. 'How do you figure that?'

Jameson handed Nash a can. 'Vicky Rollit.' He sucked the air in through his teeth. 'Piece of work that one. She's big friends with Renee Ellis, you know, that kid's mam, the boy who found your friend.'

Nash nodded, trying to keep a calm look on his face. 'She lives up the tops, right?'

'Yeah, surrounded by sheep, Pentre Halkyn, number forty-three.'

'How d'you know that?'

'I used to play darts with her old man.'

NASH HADN'T SLEPT WELL. The heat kept him awake and after that, he couldn't stop thinking. He'd dropped off at one point but was awakened by a nightmare. He dreamed about his granddad. They were at the old docks, sitting on an upturned boat. The old man was smoking a roll-up, pausing between drags to tell Nash off, pointing at him with a nicotine-stained finger. He warned Nash about Jay, telling him not to put the boy in any harm. When Nash tried to defend himself, things turned nasty. The old man accused Nash of betraying him, said he didn't care about anyone. 'How can you live with yourself,' the old man said, 'leaving your poor old granddad to rot?'

Then the old man's face changed. His eyes sunk in, and the flesh fell from his face until all that was left was his skull. It was dirt-laden and cracked. Worms wriggled out from the eye sockets and maggots swarmed over the tiny remnants of skin. The stench was awful and stayed with Nash long after he'd woken up. He brushed his teeth several times, splashed his face with cologne, but the smell lingered, settling as a foul taste in the mouth.

The dream niggled him as he drove to the tops and climbed the steep hill to Pentre Halkyn. He parked in a layby before the bus stop and walked the rest of the way. Like most places around here, Pentre Halkyn hadn't changed much. The grey, pebble-dashed bungalows were just as he remembered, as was the post office on the corner. The window display appeared unaltered, a selection of envelopes and writing pads placed incongruously beside an unopened bottle of Lucozade. Nash shook his head and smiled. This was the village time forgot, or the village of the damned more like. A snot-nosed kid riding past on his bike flicked him the V-sign. Nash met the child's stare with his own until the boy rode out of sight.

Nash made his way to number forty-three, smiling at the woman watching him from the window. Vicky Rollit opened her front door before Nash knocked. She was tall and thin, probably in her mid-thirties, although the premature grey streaked through her shoulder-length hair made her appear older. She wore a denim-blue pantsuit with red piping along the seams, and a chequered scarf around her neck. She looked smart, as though she belonged in the city, a tad over-dressed for these parts, and for the weather, too.

'Sorry to bother you,' Nash said, 'are you on your way out?'

'No, why do you ask?'

He lowered his eyes with feigned coyness. 'You look great. That colour suits you.'

'Thanks.'

Nash stared at the shine in her eyes. You'd never describe her as good-looking, but there was something there all right. A hidden gem, more noticeable when she smiled. It took years from her and, by the way she looked at him, Nash knew he was definitely her type.

He piled on the charm, complimenting her whole look, even commenting on the subtlety of her perfume. Then he cut it short. Experience taught him never to say too much.

'Listen to me going on,' he said. 'I haven't even intro-duced myself.' He offered her his hand. 'I'm Nash. I knew your cousin years ago. You probably remember me?'

As Vicky shook her head, Nash stuck with his story. 'I haven't seen your cousin for years, God rest his soul, and to be honest with you, I'm actually here on behalf of his girl-friend. She asked me to come and speak with you, pass on her condolences. She's too upset to come herself. The news came as quite a shock.'

Vicky shook Nash's hand, her palm sweaty and soft. The moment Nash mentioned her cousin, Vicky stopped smil-ing. But she didn't wear an expression of grief. Instead, she looked angry, contemptuous even. 'Yes, it's come as a shock to all of us.'

Nash remembered what the undertaker, Dafydd Benson, told him. He suppressed a smile, knowing that snippet of information was about to get him invited in. 'Your cousin's partner wants to help towards the cost of the funeral. Pay for the flowers, make a donation or something.'

Vicky's eyes widened.

'She's really cut up about it.' He flashed Vicky a sad smile. 'And as I grew up around here, she asked me to help, I couldn't say no.'

Vicky nodded. 'Sure, I understand. You best come in.'

The front room, or the lounge as Vicky called it, tried hard to emulate what every modern home aspired to be. It was a fuse of oranges and browns. The square-patterned carpet complemented the curtains. Cream-coloured skirting boards accentuated the tangerine wallpaper, and there was a spun fibreglass lampshade to match. It even had all the mod cons, a stereo system, a Phillips colour TV. The only thing spoiling it were the laced curtains. A keepsake, Nash guessed, something carried down from Vicky's childhood.

No doubt she was a tidy person. Everything was so neatly arranged, it bordered on obsession. Nash stared at the pair of Tartan slippers placed neatly under the pouffe, thinking *Here's to you, Mr. Rollit; you're doing all right.*

It seemed a nice place to retire, more so when Vicky brought in a tray of tea.

'Let me help you,' Nash said, as she eased the tray onto the coffee table. She was using her best china, keen to impress.

She nodded at the pot. 'Let it stew for a bit.'

Nash threw the room another glance. 'Lovely house you have here.'

Vicky blushed. 'I try my best. Sometimes you wonder whether it's worth it.'

He gave her a sympathetic look. 'Problems?'

Vicky shrugged. 'No more than anyone else.' Her voice

thickened. 'We were managing fine until all this stuff with my cousin George and now, apparently, we're legally obliged to pay for the funeral.' Tears welled in Vicky's eyes, and she placed her hand over her mouth.

Nash leaned forward and patted her shoulder. 'There, there, I know it's a lot to take on but try not to get upset.'

She laughed to herself. 'I'm a silly cow, sorry, embarrassing myself like that.'

'It's understandable. You're bound to be upset.' He leaned back in his chair, watching her hand shake as she poured the tea.

Vicky was growing more attractive the longer he spent with her. Some women were like that; they grew on you, looked entirely different when you studied them close up. Nash knew all about that. He was the male equivalent.

'Milk and sugar?' she said.

Nash nodded, smiling as she handed him a cup. 'Just what the doctor ordered,' he said, trying not to grimace as he took a sip.

God, the tea was bitter, it looked like something scooped up from the men's urinals. Nash placed it down on the table. 'I'll let it cool down for a bit.'

Vicky's eyes narrowed. 'You know, Mr. Nash, I think I remember you.'

'It's possible, me and your cousin were quite close. Well, when we were kids at least.'

'Was his Ex local?'

Nash paused, almost caught off guard. 'No, she's from down south. She sought me out. I hardly know her to tell you the truth.'

Vicky sipped her tea. 'And you just did her a favour, just like that?'

He fixed her with a stare. 'That's me, I'm afraid. I've always been a sucker for a pretty face.'

He saw a trace of a smile and remained silent for a moment while they exchanged glances. 'I also came to pay my respects.'

'You mean by helping with the funeral?'

Nash suppressed a smile. Vicky certainly believed in getting to the point. 'Yes, but...'

'But what?'

'She'd... she'd like something in exchange.'

Vicky slammed her cup down on the table. 'I thought it was too good to be true. Come on, what's your game? Tell us the catch.'

Her voice sounded harsh, robbed of its airs and graces. The local accent came through strong, that Liverpudlian twang from across the water, it sounded more English than Welsh. It was probably the same for most border towns. Neither fish nor fowl. Another country just a stone's throw away.

'You're mistaken,' Nash said. 'It came out the wrong way. All she wants is a keepsake. Helping towards the funeral has nothing to do with it.'

'A keepsake. What kind of keepsake?'

'I don't know, anything, I guess. She mentioned something about a watch.'

'I sold that, to the jewellers in town. I suppose you think that's a bit harsh?' She stared down at her cup. 'It was no use to me. I've got to raise the money somehow. Bob, my husband, doesn't earn too much. He has to do extra shifts.' She glanced up at him. 'I wouldn't have done it if I'd have known, Mr. Nash, honestly that's the truth.'

Nash nodded. 'You don't have to explain yourself to me. It's understandable.'

'Do you think so?'

'Absolutely, and who am I to judge.' He breathed deeply. 'I don't mean to pry, Mrs. Rollit—'

'Vicky.'

'Vicky. But did George have any other belongings?'

She shook her head with a disappointed look on her face. 'All he left was his clothes, his watch, and his wallet, and that only had a fiver. There was his car as well, but there was nothing in that except for an old suitcase.'

'Do you still have the car?'

'No. It was on its last legs. Bob sold it down the scrappy weeks ago.' She studied him for a moment. 'Your friend can have the wallet, I guess. I mean as a keepsake.'

Nash smiled. 'That's very kind of you.'

'It's the least I can do, especially as she's helping with the funeral.'

She was off again, mentioning the money at every opportunity. It never ceased to amaze Nash how money changed people. It drew the faithful into deceit, made that good friend, who you'd known for years, greedy. It didn't discriminate, turned brother against brother, mother against son. Not that Nash was any better. He knew that. He was as guilty as the rest of them.

'How much was the funeral, Vicky, if you don't mind me asking?'

'One hundred and sixty pounds.'

Nash whistled. 'They don't come cheap that's for sure.' He slipped his hand into his back pocket and took out his wallet. 'She'd like to give you half of that,' he said as he flicked through a wad of notes. He took out two twenties, a tenner, and five ones and placed them on the coffee table.

Vicky's eyes widened. 'Thanks so much,' she said and grabbed the notes from the table. She held them in her fist, her grip tightening as she drew it to her chest. Nash had half a mind to tell her that no one was about to rob her, but he thought better of it.

'I thought I had more on me. I'll have to write you a cheque for the rest.'

Vicky beamed. 'That's all right. Fifty-five's more than enough.'

'Half means half.'

'Are you sure?'

'Of course.'

Vicky's eyes brightened. 'If you insist.' She glanced down at the teapot. 'Would you like another or something stronger, perhaps?'

Nash licked his top lip. 'Yeah, why not. A cold one would be nice.'

She stood up. 'All right, I've got just the trick.'

He eyed her shape as she walked to the kitchen. She looked better from behind, long legs, a subtle sway of the hips, and a round, firm bottom to match. He pictured her naked and went hard at the thought of it.

Nash linked his hands and rested them on his lap, his arms covering his crotch. It was perfect timing because seconds later, Vicky came back in holding two cans of lager. 'Thought I'd join you,' she said. 'What the hell, all I seem to do is worry and clean this bloody house.'

She handed him a can, her hand brushing against his. Her skin felt warm and softer than he expected. He watched as she backed onto her chair, sat down, and pulled back the ring of her can. A spurt of white foam sprayed across her chest, causing her to lean forward and hold the can up to her mouth. Taking two huge gulps, Vicky caught the lager before it spilled onto her clothes.

She put the can down. 'That was close,' she said, then licked the residue from her mouth.

'You were quick,' Nash said. 'You've got good reactions.' He opened his can more carefully and raised it to Vicky. 'To George, let God have mercy on his soul wherever he might be.'

'To George,' she said.

Nash nodded, closing his eyes as he took a long swig. 'It's weird, though, don't you think?'

Vicky frowned. 'What is?'

'George, dying like that. What the hell was he thinking, a man of his age climbing up Bron Hall.'

Vicky sipped her lager. 'Who says he was thinking? He was drunk if you ask me.'

'They reckon he might have been there for weeks if that boy hadn't found him.'

'Jay Ellis.'

'Sorry?'

'That's the name of the boy who found him.'

'You know him?'

'Yeah, pretty well, I used to be a friend of the family.'

'Used to be?'

'I was big mates with his mother, Renee, until we fell out.'

Nash shook his head. 'I can't imagine you falling out with anyone.'

Vicky studied him for a moment. There was a questioning look on her face as though she was trying to decide if he was being sarcastic. To his relief, she smiled. 'I always try to be reasonable, Mr. Nash, give people the benefit of the doubt.' She smoothed a hand down the back of her hair. 'But you just can't reason with some people.'

Nash took a sip of lager. 'The boy's mother you mean?'

Vicky sighed. 'It's not so much Renee; it's *him* I've got a problem with.'

'The boy?'

'No, Jay's a good lad. I'm talking about that new bloke of hers, Shane.'

'I take it you don't like him?'

'No, I don't.' She leaned forward. 'Don't get me wrong, I'm the last person to run anyone down, but for Shane Evans, I'll make an exception.'

Nash didn't need to ask her why because Vicky, who of course was the last person to run anyone down, told him everything. She told him all about Shane Evans' reputation. 'He's done time for ABH. He's a nasty piece of work. Most people around here are afraid of him.'

Yet the thing that riled her the most was Shane's reputation with the ladies. 'He's like a dog with two dicks. He's come on to me a few times.'

'And you told Renee this?'

'Too right I did. That's what friends are for, aren't they? Not that she believed any of it.'

'I take it that didn't go down very well?'

'She went ballistic, wasn't having any of it. She called me a jealous bitch, said if anything happened, it was because of me.'

'And what did you say?'

'I told her a few home truths and I haven't spoken to her since.'

'People, huh,' Nash said and took another long swig of lager.

He placed his can down on the table, then slapped his thigh, pretending he'd just remembered something.

'What's wrong?' Vicky said.

Nash stood up. 'I didn't realise the time. I've got an appointment at one-thirty.'

Vicky glanced at the clock. 'Finish your beer. You've got plenty of time yet.'

'Nah, I best be off. It's out of town so it's quite a trek.'

Vicky looked disappointed and Nash was flattered by that.

'I'll get you George's wallet,' she said.

He placed his hand on her arm. 'There's no rush. I'll get it when I bring the cheque.'

He watched her blush, then fixed on the prickle of goosebumps spread across her neck.

The look in her eyes almost tempted him to try his luck. But he was too disciplined for that. All that talk of the mother's boyfriend gave him an idea, and he was eager to set the plan in motion. He'd keep Vicky sweet, though, just in case he needed her help.

She walked him to the front door. 'Take care,' she said.

Nash took her hand and held on to it. He squeezed her fingers and smiled. 'You take care, too. I'll call around Friday, if that's all right. It's the earliest I can make it.'

A mischievous look settled in her eyes. 'I'll be in all day, as always. Bob's in work. I have the house to myself between nine and six.'

2

SOPHISTICATED LADY

Mich was face down on the bed when the phone rang. A fat Greek businessman lay on top of her, slobbering in her ear. Straight sex and blowjobs were her usual thing, but the Greek offered her three hundred pounds for what he described as 'taking it around the back.' Mich wasn't sure at first until she saw the modest size of his manhood. He kept shouting 'Mamma, Sorry,' throughout and, once he was done, he wept.

You'd never have thought he was capable of such things when he was dressed. In his made-to-measure, pin-striped suit and his crisp white shirt with gold cufflinks, he looked so respectable. Mich learned from an early age never to take things at face value. Most people were full of crap, every look was deceptive.

The second time the phone rang she was in the shower, scrubbing herself down. It wasn't just the Greek's odour. The entire city had a stench about it, a fuse of sweat, decay, rat-infested bins, rotten drains, and sunburnt flesh. She was tired of this endless summer. She longed for the rain. This heat tainted everything.

After showering, she lay on top of the bed and this time when the phone rang, she answered.

'I've missed you,' was the first thing Nash said, which told her immediately he wanted something. He asked how she was, told her it took him several calls and three favours to get her number.

'I shouldn't be that hard to find,' she said. 'I'm an escort.' Whoring was what it really was, but neither she nor Nash mentioned it.

'You still doing that?' Nash said. 'I thought you gave it up ages ago.'

'I stopped for a while, started running a few small cons with Frank Hale.'

'How is Frank?'

'He died, from dementia.'

Nash went quiet for a moment. 'It's been nothing but bad news lately. I guess you heard about Bowen.'

Mich, as casually as she could, said, 'I heard something.'

Nash didn't answer and, in the silence that followed, she listened to the sound of his breathing. She was too tired to play games and with a deep sigh said, 'Jesus, Nash, what do you want? Spit it out.'

'Who says I want anything.'

'Why else would you be calling?'

He let out a laugh. 'I'm in a mess, Mich. Bowen cleared me out.'

'What do you mean?'

'Emptied the account, took everything.'

'Take it back then. It's no use to him now.'

'I would if I could find it.'

Mich shook her head at the phone. 'Sorry, chick, I definitely can't help you with that.'

'That's where you're wrong. In fact, to be honest with you, you're my only hope.'

MICH MADE Nash go over it several times before she gave in. She wasn't entirely convinced. But the longer Nash explained, the more the idea seemed plausible.

'And you're positive the kid's got the money?' she said.

'Absolutely, well, ninety-nine-point-nine percent.'

'What makes you so sure?'

'I just looked in the kid's eyes when I asked if he'd found anything. I know liars, Mich. I've spent nearly thirty years learning from the best of them. After I rescued him from that gang of boys, the hard-faced little thing gave me a fiver.'

'Why don't you just beat it out of him?'

Nash breathed deeply. 'He's just a kid. You know that's not my style. If it was a man, then things might be different. I can't even get close. The mother's already suspicious. Sniffing around will set off all kinds of alarm bells. No, we need to approach the situation with a bit more subtlety. There's too much counting on this. I can't afford any more mistakes. I need to gain their confidence.'

Mich lit a cigarette. 'I don't know Nash. It's a helluva lot of fuss for a gut feeling.'

'It's more than a gut feeling, but maybe five grand will persuade you.'

'Five grand?'

'Yeah, and a bit more if things go right.'

'How much money did Bowen take from you?'

'Let's not talk numbers. Let's just say it was my life savings.'

Mich took a long drag on her cigarette and slowly exhaled. She watched the smoke rise to the ceiling, then dissipate into the nicotine-stained walls. The entire room was tainted yellow, the colour of bile and sickness all around her, relentless, like the glow of the evening's sun. 'And there are no complications?'

'Nah,' Nash said. 'A standard con, just like the old days. We'll be the typical couple making new friends. I'll be the cowardly, trusting husband. You'll be the unfaithful wife.'

'What makes you think they'll go for it?'

'We'll charm them. They like to go out and drink, and most people want to be your friend when you splash money around. The mother's boyfriend will be all over you the moment he claps eyes on you. You just need to find out what he knows and hold his interest long enough for me to gain the boy's confidence.'

'And what if the kid doesn't tell you?'

'If he knows anything, he will. We've already clicked.'

Mich took another drag of her cigarette. 'Just like the old days, huh?'

'Absolutely. The only difference is I won't be stealing someone else's money. I'm taking mine back.'

'I don't know, Nash, it—'

'Come on, Mich. I want you to be up for this, on my side, helping an old friend. Please, do this willingly for me, don't force me to call in a favour.'

A knot in her stomach tightened. The bastard. She wondered how long it would take him to mention it. 'Don't threaten me, Nash.'

Nash sighed. 'Sorry, Mich, but I don't have a choice. You help me with this and it's a clean slate. Your secret stays with me.'

She closed her eyes for a second and listened to her heart pounding. 'I don't suppose I have much choice.'

'I guess not, but on the positive side, at least I'm not making you do it for free.'

MICH TOOK the train to North Wales, regretting every minute as she sat cramped in the sweat-stinking carriage. She'd forgotten it was the school holidays and the kid with the action man sitting next to her was failing miserably in appealing to her maternal instincts. He tried to get her attention, but she gave him one of her looks. The mother had no control, allowing the kid and his two younger siblings to wander around and scream and shout on a whim.

To make things worse, Mich was out of cigarettes. At least she was sat by the window, her head swimming as she looked out at the cloudless sky and the endless stretches of dead grass.

Now and then she caught glimpses of houses and smoking factories but nothing of interest. That was the trouble with travelling by train; you always saw the back end of things. The *arse of the world* as Nash described it.

Nash always had a way with words. He had a way of getting information, too, and holding on to it.

Mich grassed up Benny Bray. She didn't have a clue how Nash found this out. She didn't care either. No, all she was worried about was what would happen to her if Bray and his cronies ever got wind of it.

Almost ten years ago now but she still thought about it. Some nights fear took hold of her, plagued her mind with bad memories and created the worst scenarios. She'd been desperate. A junky whore in the wrong place at the wrong time and seen something she shouldn't have. To make things worse, she got caught shoplifting. Then someone from the CID recognised her, and it was all downhill after that: two bloated, sweaty-arsed DIs beating the shit out of her. She told them everything, even things that weren't true. During the ride home, she was forced to give one of them head and told to think of it as a bonus.

At least she wasn't sent to prison. All she ended up with was a couple of months in a rehabilitation clinic and a long list of dropped charges. God, she was so skinny back then. Heroin chic they called it, although Mich knew there was nothing stylish about it all.

A few weeks after she got out of the clinic, she came across Nash, in a bar in Soho. She hadn't seen him for years, and although he had aged little, she still noticed the change in him. She had a crush on him when she was younger, but time got rid of that. He was so confident back then, quick-witted, his every other word loaded with sarcasm. He used to make Mich laugh. But she could see why people didn't like him. She did, though. There was still something about him. Something undeniably cool.

She heard all the stories about Hilditch, young, up-and-coming, leaving Nash for dead and making him beg for his life too. She didn't know what to believe. Yet looking into Nash's eyes that day, she realised some of those stories were true. It broke her heart to see him like this. He was still Nash, of course, only less spirited, as though the fire in his belly had died, although Mich acted as though she didn't notice a thing. 'Hey stranger, long time no see. Isn't this a coincidence?'

Nash smiled, and in a voice softer than she remembered said, 'There's no coincidence, Mich. I went out of my way to find you.'

'And why would you do that?'

'Tell you the latest news about Benny Bray.'

'Benny Bray? What about him?'

'He got five years, probably be out in three.'

She tried her best to act casual, shrugging, a half-smile on her face; she had years of practice. 'And why should that interest me?'

'I just thought it would, Benny's friends are pissed off. They've started sniffing around, asking lots of questions.'

'Is that right, and what's that got to do with me?'

'Nothing yet, but perhaps it's only a matter of time. They're working their way through, speaking to everyone.'

'So?'

'Some people might let things slip, especially if they're feeling nervous, or they're offered the right price.'

'You're acting strange, Nash. I haven't got a clue what you're talking about.'

'Fine, suit yourself. I was just trying to help you that's all, advise you to lie low for a while, and tell you that your secret's safe with me.'

'What secret?'

'You know, Mich, the one about Benny Bray. The secret, that one day, might buy me a favour.'

At that moment, any sympathy Mich had for Nash melted away. He hadn't gone out of his way just to help her. Nash was too selfish for that. No, he was making it clear what he knew. That saddened her. She expected more from him. But he was no different from the rest of them.

TO DISTRACT herself from this never-ending train journey, Mich borrowed a newspaper from the guy sitting next to her. Not that it helped. Most of the headlines were about the heat, a record thirty-nine degrees in parts and showing no signs of falling.

She tried reading other articles, some nonsense about a

Cod War, a sleazy tycoon becoming president of the Seychelles. None of them held her interest.

So, resigning herself to the heat, she started doing what she did best: drawing attention to herself. She wore a white, bell-sleeved shirt dress that showed plenty of cleavage and thigh, leaving little to the imagination. There was nothing tarty about it. No matter what Mich wore, she always looked classy. She tanned quickly, her skin always smooth and fresh.

People often told her she looked like Elizabeth Montgomery, the blonde actress from *Bewitched*. Mich didn't mind that, even she saw the similarity. She was tall, beautiful, and blonde. It was difficult for most men not to be enchanted. There were exceptions, of course, with one of those being Nash.

Since their first meeting, and during those early cons, Nash kept his distance. He treated her like he treated everyone, and, unlike most men, there was no starry look in his eyes whenever they spoke. Mich liked that at first. But after a while she started having doubts. What was wrong with her?

Nash's detachment was probably one reason behind her crush, that and Nash being quite good looking, in a strange way. It soon wore off, and she realised Nash wouldn't let anyone get close.

She would try her luck sometimes, usually after she'd been drinking. Nash always knocked her back, telling her she was too good looking for him and far too young. She mentioned this to Bowen once, who told her that Nash had been a cold fish, ever since they were kids.

No, Mich-the-Witch's spells never charmed him. But that was a long time ago. She'd learned a lot since then, been through all kinds of stuff. There were other ways to deal with men like Nash.

NASH WAS WAITING for her when she finally arrived at the station. She'd never been to North Wales before, and if this station was anything to go by, she knew why.

The sign said Flint, and then Fflint, which she guessed was its Welsh equivalent. Two tower blocks loomed above the shops and houses in the distance, incongruent grey slabs marring the blue horizon.

Nash still looked the same, and she told him that as he grabbed her suitcase. She watched him as he dumped it in the boot, noticing he'd lost weight.

He flashed her a bright smile and hurried over to her with his arms wide open. She felt strange being hugged that tight, more so because he wasn't holding her out of lust but what appeared to be genuine affection.

Nash kept hold of her arms as he drew back. 'You look ace. For most people, the years can be unkind, but you just get more beautiful.'

Mich smiled. 'Looks can be deceptive,' she said. A small part of her was desperate to tell him how ugly she felt inside. But Nash probably knew that; he saw through everyone. He'd slip one day perhaps, and she'd be the one to test him. But that probably wouldn't be soon, and she abandoned the notion the moment she got in the car.

INSTEAD OF GOING DIRECTLY to Holywell, Nash took a diversion. He drove up to the tops explaining that he wanted time for a chat. 'I thought you ought to see some of the sights.'

Mich rolled her eyes. 'This place is a sight all right.'

Nash laughed, but she wasn't joking. Until now, Mich never realised how much she hated the countryside. She hated the city, too. But this was different. All there was to see were sheep, dead grass, and baked cowpats, endless desolate fields and a hazy skyline peppered with dying trees.

She hated the smell. It was worse than the city. Surely, this fetid stench was no one's idea of paradise. But mostly she hated the wide-open spaces. The vastness of it all made her nervous, a no-man's-land with a foreboding sense of dread.

She wondered how the locals coped. She would go crazy here. Not that she would stay that long. No, she'd make sure of that.

'You all right?' Nash said.

'Yeah, why?'

'Because you've got that five-thousand-yard stare in your eyes, and you've suddenly gone all quiet on me.'

'The thing is, Nash, I keep going over this little scheme of yours in my head, and each time I think about it, it seems crazier. If this kid knows where your money is, why don't you just frighten it out of him?'

Nash eased off the gas. 'I told you before, it isn't my style. He's just a kid. Also, there's still that tiny element of doubt. The kid might have found that fiver anywhere. I'm just going with my gut. You know the score, Mich, when there's even one percent of doubt, a pro needs to be careful. You can't just go charging in. That kind of approach makes things complicated.'

Mich picked up the pack of cigarettes from the dashboard and took one out. 'If you say so. It's your call, although I think my way would be easier.'

Nash let out a deep sigh. 'Listen, there's still the possibility the kid doesn't have a clue, and when people get scared, they tell you anything, make up stuff they don't know. I can't take any chances. This money is my lifeline. We need to be calm and patient. Stupid ideas mess things up. The last thing we need is to draw attention to ourselves. I've already told you; this kid doesn't scare easily.'

Mich lit her cigarette and blew the smoke over her shoulder. 'Oh, yeah, that's right, some older kids tried to hang him from a tree.' She took another drag and released the smoke through a sigh. 'Jesus, I'm looking forward to staying in this place.'

Nash laughed. 'Trust me, you don't know the half of it.'

He reached over and snatched Mich's cigarette from her hand, taking a deep drag before giving it back. 'It's not just that. If he was ever going to say anything about the money, he would have said it then, used it to bargain.'

'And you think he'll tell us?'

'Eventually, yes, once he takes me into his confidence.'

'And you think he'll do that?'

'Why not? As I told you before, we've already clicked. And who else could it be? It sure as hell isn't going to be the mother's boyfriend.'

Mich took another drag of her cigarette. 'It's a bit cruel to the kid, don't you think?'

Nash stopped smiling. 'When the hell did you get a conscience?'

'I was just saying, that's all.'

He breathed deeply. 'It's not as if he's going to come out of this with nothing. I'll see the kid right. But don't forget, it's my money.'

'All right, Nash, no need to get upset.'

'I'm not getting upset.' He pressed harder on the gas, shifted into fifth as the speedometer touched sixty. 'It'll teach him a valuable lesson.'

'And what lesson is that *Professor Nash*?'

He gave her an annoyed look. 'Life's a crock of shit, you can't trust anyone. Hell, Mich, you of all people should know that.'

Mich flicked her cigarette onto the road, feeling pleased with herself because Nash took the bait. The last word would seal the victory. 'Yeah, I guess,' she said. 'But sometimes ignorance is bliss.'

WHEN THEY ARRIVED at the B&B, Nash introduced Mich as his fiancée. The owner, a seedy old curmudgeon called Jameson, couldn't keep his eyes off her. She'd expected that, but he could have tried to make his leering a little less visible.

Whenever Jameson spoke to her, he directed most of his conversation at her tits. He slobbered a bit too, wiping his mouth with the back of his hand, leaving tiny gobbets of spit glistening across his chin. The old man smelled musty, forcing Mich to breathe through her mouth. She knew customers who smelled like that back in London, old guys mostly. Guys like Jameson, trying their best to be charming but failing at every attempt.

Jameson led them to the large double room at the back. Nash told Jameson he was all right where he was, that two singles would be okay, but the old man wasn't listening.

'But this is the best room in the house,' Jameson said. 'Ideal for couples. There's a big double bed, plenty of space and light, look,' he opened the window, 'you've even got a view of the estuary.'

Nash grew paler as he glanced across the sands. Mich had never seen him like that before. He looked vulnerable, and there was sadness in his eyes as though that remote stretch of water was drawing him to a darker place.

'Mich can have this room,' Nash said. 'She needs her rest. I keep her awake most nights with my snoring. I'm all right where I am.'

Mich watched Nash carefully as he stepped out of the room, silenced by the sudden change in him. Something about the estuary rattled him, and she wanted to know what. It was more than idle curiosity. Nash once told her how everyone was fallible, you just needed to find that chink in the armour. She held onto the thought as she followed Jameson out of the room.

'The room's lovely,' she said. 'Never mind Nash, he just likes his space.'

Jameson shrugged. 'I don't mind at all. I couldn't care less to tell you the truth.'

Mich flashed him a smile. 'I can see that, and I like someone who's their own man.'

Jameson blushed. 'I bet you've had a long journey. Would you like a drink? It's on the house.'

'I'd love to. Perhaps later. I need to freshen up first.'

'Sure, sure, of course, I didn't mean to hold you up.'

She stepped closer, her body almost touching his. 'You're not holding me up. I just want to look my best for when we have that drink.' She studied the look of desire in his eyes, forcing herself to keep a straight face. 'I best go and see my fiancé and ask him to fetch my case.'

Jameson nodded, drooling almost, a slight bulge in his trousers. Mich pretended she hadn't noticed, throwing him one last smile as she brushed past him.

. . .

WHEN SHE ENTERED Nash's room, she found him sitting on the bed staring at an open book. He looked his usual self now, poker-faced, without a care in the world.

He placed the book down on his lap and fixed his eyes on her. 'Hey, what's happening?'

'Old Jameson's got a hard-on.'

Nash laughed. 'Didn't take you long to get your hooks into him.'

'Guys like him are easy.'

'Let's hope it lasts. He's said nothing about payment.'

'Perhaps he'll let me stay for free.'

Nash shook his head. 'Believe me, there's no chance of that. You could screw that old goat all week and he'd still charge you.'

Mich smiled. 'Are you all right now?'

'What do you mean?'

'Before, in the other room, you went as white as a sheet looking at the estuary.'

'I'm all right. I don't know what you're talking about.'

Mich didn't press it. It was something to save for later. Instead, she sat next to him on the bed. 'I'm not complaining. I'm more than happy to have the room to myself.' She stretched her arms and yawned. She felt sweaty and tired, a good, long rest was what she needed. She hadn't slept well in ages. A natural sleep. A sleep unaided by tabs and booze.

Mich yawned. 'I better spruce myself up, I suppose. Mr. Jameson has invited us for a drink.'

'That's nice, but we're going to have to disappoint him.'

'Why?'

'Because we're going out.'

'Where?'

'A few of the local pubs. We've work to do, remember.

We need to find the boy's mother and her boyfriend, start getting acquainted.'

Mich sighed. 'Yeah, I guess we do. But I suppose we'll get a drink at least.'

Nash stared at her for a second. 'I wanted to speak to you about that.'

'About what?'

'Your drinking. I know it's part of the job, but I want us to keep control of this. Enjoy yourself, but let's keep any excesses down to a minimum. Any craziness can't be for real. Everything has to be an act.'

'What do you mean *any craziness can't be for real*? What are you trying to say?'

Nash sighed. 'I thought that was obvious. You know what you're like when you drink.'

Mich stood up. 'Screw you, Nash. Don't talk to me like that.'

Nash held out his hands palms up. 'I said nothing wrong, just telling you the truth that's all.'

She turned her back on him and walked out. She paused at the doorway then turned to face him. 'You need to be careful. Things can turn nasty when people talk about the truth.'

'I know, especially people like Benny Bray.'

'Go to hell, Nash,' Mich said, then walked out into the hall, slamming the bedroom door behind her. She sat on the bed and sighed into her hands. She was sick of men telling her what to do. But what sickened her more was Nash's hold over her. Perhaps after this job, he'd be true to his word. She sensed he wouldn't. Men liked to be in control. She would play along, for now, try to do as she was told, sometimes fate rewarded the patient.

3

HELLO HAPPINESS

S hane was always the same when he had no money to go out, sulking and cursing, snapping at everyone, slamming doors as he wandered in and out of the house. Jay learned to keep out of his way, and with that in mind he crept upstairs and sat on the landing, scouring the TV listings in *The Sun*.

Telly was always great on a Friday night. *It's a Knockout*, David McCallum in *The Invisible Man*, and this week, because of Wimbledon, they'd rescheduled *Starsky and Hutch*. Jay ran downstairs and told his mam, unable to contain his excitement. Shane snatched the paper from Jay's hand. 'We're not watching any of that rubbish. There's something else I want to see.'

'Such as?'

'Never you mind.'

Jay turned to his mam who was painting her toenails on the sofa. 'Tell him, Mam. I always watch my programs on a Friday night.'

Jay's mam sighed. 'Maybe Shane wants to watch something. You have to share sometimes. You can't have your own way with the telly all time.'

Jay knew that. But Shane didn't want to watch anything. The loud-mouthed prick just wanted to be awkward, taking pleasure in watching Jay get upset. But Jay was determined. He would not give him the satisfaction. No, not this time.

Ever since that day, when Nash rescued him in the woods, Jay never stopped thinking about what Nash told him: *A man needs to act smart, use his loaf to improve his situation.* Jay struggled with the idea for a while, racking his brain, trying to think of a way. Now it suddenly came to him, the idea growing stronger in his mind as he watched Shane glaring at him from the sofa.

Jay didn't respond. He just mumbled that he was off out.

'Don't be late,' his mam said without looking at him.

Jay glanced at the mantle clock on his way out. It was almost six, an hour and a quarter before *The Invisible Man*. As he stepped outside, he looked around. The avenues were quiet. They usually were on a Friday evening, everyone getting ready to go out. Even Marshall and his gang went into town, drinking cheap cans of Kestrel in the park.

Jay took the road that ran next to his house, followed it round to the back, then crossed over onto the grass bank that led to the Abbey woods. He sat down just before he reached the bottom path. He'd have to stay out for half an hour to make it look convincing. He had just under forty quid in his pocket, but he wasn't going to give Shane that much. He took out a twenty and a five and scrunched them up, then pushed them through the grass to get them dirty. He put the fiver in his pocket and placed the twenty under some grass, concealing it as best he could. Then he lay back, closed his eyes, and waited, basking beneath a dying sun.

·　·　·

JAY RAN up and down the bank a few times, building up a sweat, getting himself breathless. By the time he got back to the house, he could barely speak.

'What's wrong, Jay?' his mam said. 'Calm down.'

'Money,' Jay shouted, 'found it just now, in the woods.'

The instant Jay showed them the five-pound note Shane stood up. He snatched the fiver from Jay's hand and held it up to the window. 'It's a real fiver, all right. Where the hell did you find it?'

Jay caught his breath, exaggerating it for effect. 'D-down the bank, just before the woods.'

'Was there anymore?'

Jay shrugged. 'Dunno.'

Shane rested a hand on Jay's shoulder, his tone softening as he said, 'You best show me where you found it, see if there's anymore.'

Jay nodded, waiting by the front door while Shane slipped on his sandals.

They hurried round to the back, Jay taking the lead with Shane close behind. Before they reached the bottom of the bank, Jay pointed at a heap of dried grass then watched as Shane crouched down and started searching.

Shane was like a man possessed and reminded Jay of one of those guys from the old cowboy films frantically searching for gold. Shane punched the air. 'Sound as,' he shouted, and, just as he had done with the fiver, he held the twenty-pound note to the light.

Shane shook his head and, with a big smile on his face, said, 'I can't believe it.'

He shoved the twenty into his pocket and resumed rummaging through the grass. Jay helped, feigning excitement. When Shane stood up and said to call it a day, Jay carried on searching.

'Leave it,' Shane said. 'There's nothing else there. I'm not complaining. Twenty-five quid'll do me.'

Jay got up. 'But some of that's mine, right?'

Shane looked at him for a second, then ruffled Jay's hair. 'Of course, don't worry. As soon as I get some change, I'll see you right.'

Of course, you won't, you liar, Jay felt like telling him but smiled instead.

They walked back to the house side by side as though they'd been buddies for years. Shane was whistling a tune, 'Hello Happiness', by *The Drifters*. Before they reached the gate, they saw Marshall and his cronies walking past the bus stop. Marshall was loud as usual but fell silent the moment he saw Shane. Shane pointed at Marshall. 'Me and you are going to catch up real soon. You can bet your life on it.'

Jay expected Marshall to say something but all he did was look away.

'You stay clear of Jay,' Shane shouted after him. 'The same goes for your poofy little mates, too.'

Jay glanced up at Shane, unable to stop smiling as Shane said, 'I'll sort that dickhead out tomorrow. Don't you worry anymore about him.'

As they strolled up the garden path, Jay's mam watched them from the window. She opened the front door, an expectant look on her face. 'Well?'

Shane grinned. 'I'll tell ya inside. I don't want the entire street knowing our business.'

She followed Shane into the living room, leaving Jay to close the front door. The moment the door slammed shut, Shane let out a tremendous roar of delight. 'We've hit the jackpot, Renee. Tart yourself up because you and me are off out.'

Jay watched him from the hall. Shane stood with his legs

slightly apart, sticking his chest out, a note in each hand, waving them in front of Jay's mam as though he'd won a fortune. He caught Jay staring, then turned to Jay's mam and said, 'Renee, give the boy that quid you were saving. I promised I'd see him right.'

Jay's mam looked at him and winked. 'Appears everyone's luck's in.' She grabbed her purse from the side table, opened it, and handed Jay a crumpled one-pound note.

Shane flashed him a smile. 'Get a load of fish and chips and buy yourself one of those horror books from Woolies you like reading.'

'I go to the library these days,' Jay said.

Shane dropped his smile. 'Oh, aye, what are ya reading?'

'Charles Dickens, *Great Expectations*.'

Shane laughed. 'Aren't you the brainbox. Saw the film of that once, boring as shite.'

'It's not boring at all. I like the—'

'Whatever. I need to get ready. We'll talk about it later, yeah.'

Jay nodded. 'Okay, but when do I get the rest of my fiver?'

That mean look returned to Shane's eyes, but it only settled there for a moment. 'I'll give it to your mam later. She'll add it to your savings.' He ruffled Jay's hair then gently shoved him to one side.

'Don't you worry, Jay,' his mam said. 'I'll make sure he gives me that money.'

Jay thanked her with a smile, knowing neither of their promises would come true.

EVERYTHING TURNED OUT AS PLANNED, and Jay felt pleased with himself. There was a friendly atmosphere in the house for once, Shane singing at the top of his voice, Jay's mam giggling as she scampered across the landing; he'd have to get them out of the house more often.

Jay lay belly-down on the carpet, one eye on his book and the other on the TV. The *Invisible Man* didn't start until quarter past seven, so that gave him just under twenty-five minutes to read a few more pages. He was on chapter seven already, but he was re-reading chapter one, the part where Pip first meets Magwitch. The way Dickens described the marshes reminded Jay of the estuary. He'd started taking walks there again. A few weeks ago, as he roamed the estuary path, he imagined himself finding a stranger. An escaped convict just like Magwitch. Never in his wildest dreams did Jay think he'd actually come across one. He pictured the stranger's face and that moment when the stranger's eyes fixed on his. There had been a fearful look in the man's eyes, forcing Jay to turn away, and Jay was making his way back to the road when he'd heard the man fall.

Jay shut his eyes for a second and cast the image of the dead man aside, closing his book as his mam blocked the TV.

She twirled in front of him. 'Well, how do I look?'

As was always the case whenever she dressed up, Jay thought she looked fantastic. She smelled great too. But there was something more about her this evening, a fresh-ness in the eyes, a youthful glow in her tanned cheeks. She looked like his mam of old. A person he hadn't seen in ages. She was wearing a pair of new jeans, and a tight turquoise vest decorated with coloured sequins. She wore her hair down, its auburn sheen matching the green-brown hues of her eyes.

'Say something then,' she said. 'Don't just lie there gawping.'

'You look beautiful,' Jay said.

His mam blushed, and he could feel his cheeks redden too. Thankfully, the uncomfortable moment was short-lived, the brief, awkward silence broken by Shane swaggering into the living room. He slapped Renee's backside. 'Come on, sexy, let's go. I'm itching to get out.'

'Patience,' she said and reached out to Jay and pulled him up. She wrapped her arms around his waist and held him close to her chest. 'You keep safe, Jay. Go to Garney's for your fish 'n chips. I don't want you hanging around town.'

'He'll be fine,' Shane said. 'He's not a baby.'

She held Jay tighter. 'He is to me.'

Jay pulled away. 'I'm thirteen, Mam.'

His mam looked into his eyes and smiled, her voice tender as she said, 'That isn't very old you know.'

Jay feigned relief as she released him, but secretly he could have stayed in her arms all night. He walked with them outside, following as far as the gate. He watched them walk up Moor Hill, a pang of loneliness aching inside him as the humid, evening air carried their laughter.

AT FIRST, Jay thought he was in a dream, listening to everyone's laughter, watching his mam and another woman dance. He hadn't seen the woman before. All he knew was that she looked amazing, like a film star or someone you'd expect to see on TV. As he turned his head slightly, he noticed Nash was in the room too, playing three-card brag with Shane at the corner table. Shane was holding a can of lager, pointing it at the air as he spoke at the top of his voice. 'I've always voted Labour me, but this shower of shite is ballsing up everything.'

Nash opened his mouth to say something but kept silent

as he fixed his eyes on Jay. 'Hey little fella. Did all our noise wake you up?'

Jay shook his head, feeling self-conscious as everyone looked at him. He sat up, yawning as he stretched his arms. 'I must have fallen asleep.'

Shane laughed. 'That's an understatement. You've been snoring like a pig for ages.'

'Leave him alone,' the stranger-woman said. 'He looked lovely curled up on the sofa. I wish to God I could sleep like that.'

Jay stared at the woman, silenced by her beauty. He couldn't keep his eyes off her and kept watching her until Nash got up from his chair and walked towards him.

Nash crouched in front of Jay. 'Nice to see you again, bud.'

Jay glanced at his mam.

'It's okay Jay,' she said. 'As you can see, we're all friends now.'

Nash smiled. 'We are indeed, and we have this little fella to thank for the party.'

Jay frowned. 'What do you mean?'

Nash fixed his eyes on him. 'It seems you've got the luck of the Irish. You're a right little gold magnet.'

'Too right he is,' Shane shouted. 'I'm taking him back down there tomorrow.'

Nash picked up Jay's book from the carpet, then sat next to him on the sofa. He flicked through the pages, read a couple of sentences under his breath, then put the book face down on his lap. 'I love Dickens. This is one of my favourites.'

'Why's that?' Jay said, delighted Nash had shown an interest.

Nash looked Jay in the eye. 'You know what it's about, right?'

Jay nodded. 'Of course, I do. It's about bettering yourself.'

'Kind of,' Nash said. 'But at what cost, and at who's loss. It takes a while before Pip gets a conscience, living the high life, spending money that isn't his.'

Jay blushed, and he could feel his heart pounding in his chest. Yet, before he could think of an answer, Shane spoke over him. 'Listen to the Professor over there. Hey, Nash, did you just swallow an encyclopaedia?'

Nash looked at Shane. 'No, just enjoy reading.'

Shane laughed. 'I've never been interested in books.'

'Oh, I can see that.'

Shane stood up and flicked open a can of lager, spraying the foam towards Nash. 'Are you trying to say I'm stupid or something?'

Nash didn't answer, and suddenly the room felt so quiet. The record finished. Jay's mam and the blonde woman stopped dancing. Shane kept staring, and this time Jay could feel his heart beating inside his chest. He suddenly realised how warm it was. The stale muggy air was stifling. He tried to swallow the dryness in his throat; the knots in his stomach tightened as they always did when Shane was about to kick off.

'That's not what I meant,' Nash said. 'I'm sorry if that's how it came across.'

Shane took a big swig of lager, part of it dribbling down his chin. He studied Nash for a second. 'You need to watch what you're saying. We're a touchy lot around here, quick to take things the wrong way.'

Nash mumbled something beneath his breath.

Shane stepped forward. 'What was that?'

'Nothing,' Nash said. He held out his hands, but before he could say anything else, the blonde woman stood in front of him. She fixed her eyes on Shane. 'Hey, come on. Nash told you he didn't mean anything. Let's slip another record on and have a dance. This is supposed to be a party.' The blonde woman wiggled her hips and danced towards him. She looked sexy and funny, and even Shane found it hard not to laugh.

Nash stood and offered Shane his hand. 'Sorry,' he said, his voice sounding nervous.

Shane gripped Nash's hand. 'Apology accepted, but next time Prof, you be careful. I'm not the guy to give people second chances.'

'I can tell that,' Nash said. 'I'm sorry, Shane. I won't make that mistake again.'

Nash turned to face Jay and winked, then tapped the side of his head. Jay nodded slightly and smiled. He knew exactly what Nash was telling him.

A man needs to use his loaf.

NASH MIGHT NOT HAVE BEEN as tough as Shane, but he was definitely more fun. It had been over a week now since Nash and his fiancée, Mich, had first come back to Jay's house. During that time, they'd visited most days, and went drinking in town with Shane and Jay's mam almost every night. Jay liked that, not just because most evenings he had the house to himself, but he loved spending time with Nash.

Two days ago, they'd taken Jay out too. Letting him sit in the front of Nash's car as they drove to Rhyl. They took him to the Fun-Fair, filled his belly with chips and hot dogs. He'd felt so alive walking along the promenade, the warm air thick with the smell of sand, candyfloss, and fried onions.

He loved the glitter of the sea, the whiz and the whirr from the arcades, and the top-twenty hits blaring through pub windows. All these things made him feel happy and sad at the same time, his enjoyment scarred slightly by momentary feelings of loss. He figured Nash sensed this because when Shane suggested they go to the pub, Nash shook his head and said, 'Nah, I'll give it a miss. You guys go and have a few beers. I'll take a walk along the beach with my buddy here.'

They carried their shoes and socks and walked barefoot across the warm sand. The waves washed back and forth on the shore and Jay asked if the tide was coming in or out.

'In,' Nash said, 'but don't worry, bud, there's plenty of time yet.'

'Are you sure?'

Nash smiled. 'Yeah, why do you ask?'

'The tide comes in pretty quick around here, especially down the estuary. You can stand on the sands one minute,' Jay clicked his fingers, 'and there's water all around you the next.'

Nash pointed to the promenade steps. 'We can walk along the top if you like.'

Jay shook his head. 'Nah, it's all right. I was just saying, that's all.'

'No need to apologise, bud. I like your style. It's wise to question people.'

Those words wrapped themselves around Jay's heart like a warm glove. He didn't answer, savouring the feeling for a good ten minutes. When he spoke, his voice seemed softer, and he felt calm inside as he pointed at the horizon shining gold beneath a low sun. 'That's the Irish Sea, and beyond it is the Atlantic, then America. I'm going there one day.'

He paused, waiting for Nash to tell him to shut up, just

as his mam and Shane did whenever he got excited. Yet Nash just stared at him, a look of deep concentration in his eyes. 'You'll need a bit of money to do that, bud.'

'How much do you reckon?'

Nash stopped and took out his pack of cigarettes. He popped one in his mouth, flicked open his lighter, and cupped his hands around the flame. He took a deep drag of his cigarette, then snapped the lighter shut, squinting as he considered the question. A waft of smoke preceded him as he spoke. 'Dunno, a couple of thousand at least, more probably. But you'll have to work hard for years to save that much.'

'Perhaps not,' Jay said, regretting his words the moment they left his mouth.

Nash took a drag of his cigarette and blew the smoke over his shoulder. 'What do you mean, *perhaps not*? Have you got a secret hoard stashed away or something?'

Jay's heart beat faster. The knot in his stomach tightening as he tried to think of something to say. He shook his head. 'No, I mean it might not take as long as that.'

Nash fixed him with a stare. 'Oh, I think it would unless you were earning big money or won the pools or something.' He nodded towards a boy playing with a bucket and spade in the sand. 'Perhaps we should take a leaf out of his book and start digging, see if we can find any treasure.'

Jay's throat felt dry as he swallowed. 'There's no treasure here.'

'You'd be surprised, bud, what some people lose, and others find.'

Jay held Nash's stare with his own. 'What would you do with the treasure if you found any?'

'That's a good question. I'd keep it I suppose, wait awhile

till no one claimed it, then buy Mich and me a nice place, a new car, share some of it with you.'

Try as he might, Jay couldn't hide his smile. 'Honest?'

'Honest, we're best buddies. You'd do the same for me, right?'

'Of course,' Jay said, and a part of him meant it.

'That's good to hear, and God knows I could do with some luck.'

'Why?'

Nash stubbed out his cigarette. 'I'm broke, bud, but you have to swear to keep it between you and me. Cross your heart and hope to die. It'll be our secret.'

Jay nodded.

'You know why I came back here, right?'

'Mam said it was to do with that guy, the one I found in the woods. You're doing a favour for a friend of his.'

'That's partly true. But it's not the real reason. Between you and me, bud, I'm broke, lost my job a few weeks ago. Of course, I wanted to help my friend out, but that's only half of it. I came back here to get away, think things through, who knows, I might even get a job.'

'There isn't much work around here, only Courtauld's factory.'

Nash momentarily placed a hand over his mouth and made a strange noise and Jay wondered if it was to suppress a cry. 'I know, bud, things are looking pretty grim. But like I said, let's keep this between you and me. I'm using the last of our savings to give Mich a little holiday. She'd worry herself to death if she knew the truth.' He ruffled Jay's hair. 'It could be worse, huh? At least we're alive, unlike the poor fella you found in the woods.'

Jay nodded, keeping his eyes fixed on the sand.

'I bet that shook you up a bit,' Nash said, 'finding him like that.'

Jay shrugged. 'Sort of, I try not to think about it.'

'That's the best way. Focus on what's ahead. Keep a positive attitude.' Nash took a deep breath. 'I need to do the same. A man needs to make his own luck.' He threw Jay a wink. 'And who knows, you might be my lucky charm. You're a right little treasure magnet from what Shane tells me.'

Jay felt his body stiffen. 'What did he say?'

'That you found over twenty quid down the woods.'

'That was just a one off.'

Nash studied him for a moment. 'Let's hope not, hey.'

DURING THE RIDE HOME, Jay couldn't stop feeling guilty. He felt sorry for Nash, and as he watched the night sky slowly darken, he considered giving him some money and telling him the truth, perhaps. Even when he dozed off, guilt tainted his dreams, every image and every shadow was laden with a heavy heart.

When they arrived back home, Jay pretended to be asleep, and Nash carried him back to the house. He liked that; he felt safe in Nash's arms. That night, Nash and Mich stayed over. Jay loved that, too, especially when his mam and Shane went to bed, and Mich fell asleep. He had Nash all to himself. They sat together on the sofa watching the late film on TV. It never ceased to amaze Jay how Nash could predict a movie's ending. He was the same with other programmes too, sometimes knowing what the actors were going to say next. When Jay asked him how he knew, Nash smiled and tapped the side of his nose. 'Just a knack I've always had. It doesn't pay for a man to tell people all his secrets.'

Jay liked the sound of that. In fact, he liked most things Nash said, and the way he said them, too. Nash had a calming presence about him. There was a kindness about him that Jay didn't see in most people. He loved the way Nash dressed. He was always clean and tidy. He smiled a lot and was always punctual. Jay liked Mich too, of course, but for other reasons. She was the most beautiful woman he'd ever seen. He hinted at this to his mam once by asking if Mich had ever been a film star. His mam appeared annoyed by this.

'No, not to my knowledge, although, I can see why you might think that by the way she flaunts herself.'

Jay's mam passed a lot of comments like that. She'd be off with Mich sometimes, and whenever Mich spoke with Shane, especially for long periods of time, she'd always interrupt. Jay asked her why she kept doing it. But all she told him was that he was too young to understand, and he should mind his own business. Nash was the complete opposite. He was happy to share everything. As though every aspect of his life was Jay's business.

'You come and talk to me whenever you want, Jay,' Nash kept reminding him. 'If there's anything on your mind, or something's troubling you, come and see me. Sometimes it's good to get things off your chest, and I'm no blabber mouth. I know how to keep a secret.'

JAY HATED WEDNESDAYS, almost as much as he hated Sundays. Wednesdays felt listless and long. The shops had a half-day closing and there was never anything good on TV.

He tried fighting the boredom by walking down to the estuary, and that was where he met the stranger.

Jay didn't like the look of him from the off. He just stood there staring. It was a creepy look, and he reminded Jay of those guys they warn kids about in the public information films. He dressed the part too. He wore a grubby, sweat-stained shirt, and the jacket of his grey flannel suit was slung over his shoulder. His trousers were too short, revealing his off-white, towelling socks. The man's shoes were no better, dusty black winkle pickers, with laces so tight they looked ready to snap. Yet what caught Jay's attention the most was the man's hands. The skin was calloused and pale. The nail of each bony, nicotine-stained finger was bitten down to a stub. 'What are ya up to, kid?'

Jay looked on in silence, struggling to match the man's skinny, Oriental appearance with the deep, southern accent. 'What are ya up to, I said? What's the matter, cat got your tongue?'

Jay shook his head.

'Answer me then. Don't you know it's rude not to speak when someone asks you a question.'

Jay frowned. 'I don't know you, and Mam said never to talk to strangers.'

The man took a step forward, causing Jay to take two steps back.

'Nervous little tyke, aren't yer.'

'Not really, just cautious that's all.' Jay tapped the side of his head. 'A man needs to use his loaf.'

The man's eyes brightened as though a match had just been struck behind them. 'That's an odd turn of phrase for a boy of your age. There's a very good friend of mine, the man I'm looking for, who always says that. A man called Nash.'

'How good a friend?' Jay said.

The man grinned. 'I'd say he was my best friend.'

Jay clenched his fists and fixed his eyes on him. 'He never mentioned—'

'Oh, so you know him then?' The man straightened.

'Might do, who's asking?'

'Pete.'

'He's mentioned nothing about any *Pete*.'

'Perhaps he doesn't tell you everything.'

Jay glared at him. 'How come you came looking for him down the estuary?'

'I've been walking everywhere, asking around. Someone said they saw a man fitting Nash's description walking with some kid down the estuary, so I thought I'd take my chance.'

'That's a bit lucky.'

'Not really, kid, I've been up and down here for hours. You must be about the twentieth person I've asked.'

Jay remained silent, fearing he'd already said too much. As Pete talked, it became clear that he wasn't as stupid as he looked.

'So where is he then?' Pete said.

Jay shrugged. 'In the B&B, I suppose.'

'Which B&B?'

'The big blue house, before you get to the fire station.'

Jay ran off before Pete could answer. He heard Pete calling after him, that deep southern accent fading as he gained more distance.

JAY RUSHED BACK to see if he could find Nash first and tell him the big news. He popped into his house on the way to check in on his mam. He found her stretched on the sofa smoking a cigarette. She'd been mooching around the house for days now, ever since Shane announced he was going to renovate his auntie's old bungalow. Shane's auntie left him the place in her will. Jay had only been there once and thought it looked a bit of a sight. Most of the windows were boarded over, slates were missing from the roof, and someone sprayed graffiti across the back door. The garden looked a mess: bin bags everywhere, dog ends and empty beer cans scattered across the overgrown lawn. The bungalow was situated up in the tops, nestled near the woods, hidden among the fields, woods, and dark country lanes that led to isolated tiny villages. Jay didn't enjoy going to the tops. They spoke Welsh there, and although it was only six miles from town, it felt like another country.

Jay's mam was the complete opposite. Initially, she'd been excited by the idea and begged Shane to let her help. Shane refused, insisting he wanted to keep it as a surprise. He also made them promise not to mention it to anyone in case they stopped his dole money. Jay's mam persisted for a while, sometimes she wouldn't stop going on about it.

'You'll see it when it's finished,' Shane kept telling her. 'I'm losing patience now, so I don't want to hear any more about it.'

That was enough to keep her quiet, but she'd been sulking ever since.

Jay liked Shane being out of the house all day. It meant he had his mam to himself. He'd tried to snap her out if it, but there was no getting through to her. She seemed worse today, sighing every other minute as she stared blankly at the TV. She sounded slurry when she spoke, and Jay guessed she was back on the tablets. He hated it when she took Valium 'mother's little helper', as they called it. It made her act like a dope, slurring her words, burning the tea. Last year it got so bad his mam's ex-boyfriend, Stan, hid the tablets from her, and he forced her to be sick and held her head over the toilet.

She'd been doing well for some time until all this stuff about Shane's bungalow. She even started refusing to go out, and the last few nights Shane went out alone.

'Yeah, off you go,' she'd shouted after him. 'Go and see that stuck-up, blonde slut.'

Jay couldn't figure out why his mam hated Mich so much. Mich was polite, funny, and kind, with nothing but good things to say. She complimented Jay's mam a lot, but Jay's mam often took it the wrong way. When Jay asked his mam why she acted like that, she told him he was too young to understand. But he understood all right. He didn't blame his mam for being jealous. But he hated it when she became so needy. That's what she was today, and it saddened him to see her like this.

Jay tried to cheer her up. 'It's lovely outside, Mam. I'm going to see Nash. You can come with me if you like.'

She didn't answer him at first, then, in a slurred and distant voice, said, 'Nash? What the bloody hell do I want to see him for? I've got better things to do. You spend too much time with him. You should find some friends your own age.'

Jay kept on at her. He wasn't going to give up that easily. He commented on the TV, predicted the plot lines, trying to be smart and funny like Nash, but when his words had no effect, he tried changing the subject. 'What would you do if you won the pools, Mam?'

His mam raked her fingers through her hair and sighed. 'I dunno, buy a house I suppose.'

'Where?'

'Anywhere, as long as it's a million miles away from here, and not some dilapidated old bungalow up the tops.'

Jay liked the sound of that and almost told her she could

have any house she wanted. It came with a condition of course, they could go anywhere, do anything, providing it didn't include Shane and providing they could help Nash. Jay felt it was time to move on. What was the point in having all that money if he couldn't use it; it wasn't any good to anyone hidden away? But he needed to be sure and tested the water. 'That sounds great, Mam. I'd like that, a big house looking out onto the sea, no one living there except me and you.'

She didn't answer, so he said it again. Louder this time, which forced her to open her eyes. 'What? What are you mythering about now?'

'I'm not mythering, Mam. I just said I liked the idea of me and you living in a beautiful big house.'

'Yeah, it's nice to dream. But even if we could afford it, Shane would never move. He loves it around here. He'd live nowhere else.'

'Who said anything about Shane? It would be just you and me.'

Her eyes widened. 'I couldn't go anywhere without Shane. He's the love of my life. My soulmate.' She started crying then, a deep, self-indulgent sob. Jay watched her in silence, fighting back his tears, pitying her, and hating her at the same time. *Forget Shane*, he wanted to say. *Sort yourself out. I'm your son. What about me?* But he didn't say a thing. Instead, he stood up and sloped off into the hall, the emptiness growing inside him as he opened the front door.

It was a horrible feeling, a mixture of sadness and dread, intensified by every step, consuming him as he walked up Moor Hill. He kept his head down and would have marched past Nash without even noticing him if Nash hadn't blocked his way. 'Hey, bud, what's the rush?'

Jay sighed. 'Nothing,' he said, then shook his head.

Nash studied him for a moment. 'It doesn't look like *nothing* to me.'

Jay shrugged. 'I just got a few things on my mind that's all.'

Nash placed a hand on Jay's shoulder. 'Come on, let's go for a walk and you can tell me all about it.'

They headed towards the valley woods. Neither of them said a word for the first ten minutes, partly because of the heat from a high, midday sun blazing down on them. They found a brief respite among the trees and stopped to catch their breath. Even in the shade it felt hot. The temperature rose every day and showed no sign of easing. Hosepipe bans were now the law of the land, and Jay heard them talking on the news about appointing a *Minister for Drought*. He wasn't sure what such a minister would do. Not that he cared. He had too many problems of his own to think about.

Jay shielded his eyes with his hand and looked towards the Flour Mill pool glimmering in the distance, then let out a heavy sigh. He heard the snap of Nash's lighter and watched Nash take a drag of his cigarette, his eyes following a thin cloud of smoke as it drifted above the trees.

'For someone who's supposed to be all right,' Nash said, 'you certainly don't look it.'

Jay looked at Nash and smiled then told him all about it. He didn't mention his mam's past troubles, only that she was taking tablets. He said nothing about Mich either. Mostly he focused on the conversation he'd had with his mam about their dream house.

Nash didn't say a word throughout. He just stood there and listened. Once Jay was finished, Nash dropped his cigarette onto the ground and stubbed it out with the heel of his shoe. He toed it deeper into the dust. 'Got to make sure. A few stray sparks and the whole woods will be on fire.' He fixed his eyes on Jay. 'I can see why you get frustrated with your mam. But she thinks the world of you. It doesn't take a genius to see that.'

'You wouldn't think so, though, especially by the way she acts.'

Nash nodded. 'Yeah, I know. But like most grown-ups, she has her problems.'

'She doesn't seem happy unless she has problems. Most of the time, I think she creates them.'

'What makes you say that?'

Jay glanced down the valley towards the trees. 'She thinks Shane's having an affair with Mich.'

'Hmm, jealousy's a terrible thing.'

'You can say that again. As if Mich would ever be interested in *him*.'

'You don't like Shane very much, do you?'

'No, I don't. I think he's a bullshitting prick, don't you?'

Nash laughed. 'He's a bit of character that's for sure. But he isn't that bad.'

Jay frowned. 'How can you say that, especially the way he talks to you?'

'He's only having a bit of a laugh.'

'No, he's not. He's poking fun at you, calling you Professor all the time. He's trying to make you look small in front of Mich.' Jay looked down at the ground. 'I know it's difficult to say anything. Shane's hard, most people fear him.'

'I'm not afraid of him, Jay. I just don't like trouble, that's all. I'm like you. I want a nice life.' He let out a deep sigh. 'That big house by the sea, the one you mentioned before. I tell ya, if I had the money, I'd buy you that house today. In fact, me and Mich would probably move in with you.'

'Do you mean that?'

'Of course I do.' Nash picked up a stick and swung it towards the trees. 'But like I told you before, I'm broke, so there's no chance of that. But there's no harm in dreaming, huh?'

'No, there isn't, but sometimes dreams come true.'

Nash looked at him and smiled. 'You believe that don't you?'

'Of course.'

'What makes you so sure?'

Jay studied him for a moment. He wanted to confess. He would have loved nothing more than to tell Nash everything. That tiny voice inside him held him back. He didn't know what to do. He couldn't keep it a secret forever. He needed to trust someone. Why shouldn't that someone be Nash? Jay took a deep breath. 'Nash...'

'Yeah?'

'Can I tell you something?'

'Of course you can, bud. You can tell me anything. You know that.'

'If I tell you something important, do you promise not to get angry, and that you'll keep it secret? I mean we're friends, right?'

'Cross my heart and hope to die. We're best friends.'

Jay smiled. Then his eyes widened as he suddenly remembered the big news he wanted to share with Nash. 'I thought Pete was your best friend?'

'Pete?'

'Yeah, Pete.'

'I don't know anyone called Pete.'

'He knows you, said you and him go way back.'

'What? When?'

'Today, I saw him down the estuary this morning. He

asked me if I knew you. He said he'd spent hours looking for you.'

Nash shook his head and smiled. 'What did he want?'

'Just asked if I knew you, where you were. Other than that, he didn't say.'

'And you told him where I was, right?'

Jay looked down at the ground. 'I didn't mean to say anything, but he riled me a bit. Then it was too late, so I ran off.'

'What did this Pete look like?'

'A creepy, skinny, little fella, with greasy hair, sort of Chinese looking.'

'Yeah, that sounds like Pete, all right.'

Nash's reaction surprised Jay. He thought he would have been pleased. But he looked shocked at first and now a little angry. Jay watched Nash stare into space, then, as though realising he was miles away, Nash broke into a smile. 'That's good news, bud. Now what was it you wanted to tell me?'

Jay changed his mind. He'd tell him about the money another time. He'd come this far without saying a word to anyone. Why risk everything now? Nash seemed rattled and had that look about him. Jay noticed it now and then. That steely eyed distance that made him look like someone else. It wasn't the Nash Jay knew. No, it was someone meaner.

Jay shrugged. 'It doesn't matter. I don't want to talk about it now.'

'Are you sure? You know, sometimes it pays to get things off your chest before they eat away at you.'

Jay forced a smile. 'Maybe, but I'd rather tell you about it later.'

Nash ruffled Jay's hair. 'No problem, bud. I'm always here for you, remember that.'

4

THIS MASQUERADE

Nash was angry, just when he was making progress with Jay, forces beyond his control seemed set on ruining everything. It wasn't just the sudden arrival of Pete that bothered him, he was having problems with Mich too. He'd told her to reel Shane in and find out what he knew, and now that it was obvious Shane didn't have a clue, there was no need for Mich to spend so much time with him. Instead of doing what she was told, she did the opposite, shacking up with Shane every day in that old, shabby bungalow.

'A girl's got to have some fun in this shithole of a town,' she said when Nash questioned her about it. 'Shane loves me. He's obsessed with me. He'd do anything I ask.'

'Is that right,' Nash said. 'You should take him back to London with you then. Perhaps he can sort all that mess with Benny Bray out for you.'

That shut her up, but only for a bit. 'Perhaps I should.'

'Or maybe you shouldn't,' Nash said. 'He's a prick. He just doesn't know it yet.'

'He's not soft you know. He's got a bit of a reputation.'

'Yeah, in a one-street town. You take that little fish out of its pond, and he'll be squirming and gasping for air like the rest of them.'

'I thought maybe he could join us.'

Nash shook his head.

'Why not? He could be useful. Jay's scared of him. He'd tell Shane where the money was with a little persuasion.'

'No.'

'But you're not making much progress. Shane could—'

Nash slammed his fist into the wall. 'I said no. Shut it, Mich. Don't mention it again.'

'All right, all right, keep your shirt on.'

Nash took a deep breath. 'Jay will tell me in his own time. In fact, he almost did today, until Pete-the-Chink spoiled everything.'

'Pete-the-Chink? What the hell's he doing here?'

Within a few moments of mentioning Pete's name, there was a knock on Nash's bedroom door. Nash reached for his cigarettes as Mich stood up and opened the door. Nash knew it was Pete straight away by the sudden waft of Brylcreem. There was a strong smell of sweat too, but in this weather, everyone was guilty of that. Pete flashed them a nicotine-stained smile. 'Congratulations on your engagement. I never realised you two were so close.'

Nash took a drag of his cigarette. 'What do you want, Pete?'

Pete feigned a look of surprise. 'Who says I want anything?'

Nash sighed and stood up. 'Let's go for a walk. Just you and me. If you're going to soil the air with your bullshit, I recommend you do it outside.'

. . .

THEY TOOK a walk down the level, a hilly stretch of grassland where, years ago, they used to mine for lead. Two of the mines were still there, but the council had filled them with rocks and debris. The old mine cart tracks were barely recognisable. Most of them were buried beneath the hard, flattened earth and used as footpaths. A stream trickled down the right bank, tapering off as it ran next to the lower path. At least there was some shade here, provided by a thicket of small trees. The trees were fenced off and a large wooden sign said: PRIVATE. KEEP OUT.

Nash leaned against the fence and took out his pack of cigarettes. He held the box towards Pete and Pete snatched one out.

'Thanks,' Pete said. 'I ran out about half an hour ago. I haven't had the chance to buy any.'

He popped the cigarette into his mouth and Nash gave him a light. Pete drew hard on it, as though he were a condemned man, and the cigarette was his last. Finally, he plucked it from his mouth and released the smoke. 'I needed that. Burns the chest, though. I never enjoy a smoke as much in this heat.'

Nash fixed his eyes on him, watching the gaunt, jaundiced face flash him a weak smile. Nash hated that smile, and it took all his effort not to slap it off.

'Why are you looking at me like that?' Pete said. 'You're making me nervous.'

'I very much doubt that, Pete. You've never struck me as the nervous type.'

'What's wrong then?'

'Nothing, just waiting for you to get to the point and tell me what you want.'

'Who says I want anything?'

Nash moved away from the fence. 'I'm not in the mood

for games.' He started walking down the path and could hear the lightness of Pete's tread behind him.

The path filtered out onto the bottom of the Well Hill. Nash stopped when he reached the pavement, staring at the Holy Well of St. Winefride's on the other side of the road. He crossed over to take a closer look, Pete following him through the rusty turnstile.

Nash hadn't been here since he was a kid. Back then he never used the main entrance, he always climbed over the fence. This was the first time he'd strolled down the main walkway. As far as he could see nothing had changed. But the place still felt new to him. The main bathing pool still looked the same, the water an icy green-blue, with a scattering of copper and silver coins glinting from its base. Even the shrine's entrance was unaltered, a tripartite of stone archways, dark and strangely menacing, the bubbling spring faint among the candle-lit shadows.

Preferring to watch the well from a distance, Nash sat on a bench. Pete sat beside him and glanced around. 'I'm a bit confused, to be honest, Nash. I would have thought they'd name this town after this place, but when I arrived here yesterday, I noticed the sign read "Welcome to HolyHell."'

Nash smiled to himself. 'Someone's idea of a joke.'

Pete sucked the air through his teeth. 'Perhaps, but many a true word is spoken in jest.'

Nash gave him a sidelong glance. 'I'm only going to ask you this once more. Why did you come here?'

'I came to see you.'

'Why?'

'You've been here for a few weeks now. I was getting worried about you, wondering what you were up to.'

'I'm not up to anything. Just came here to pay my respects to Bowen and his family, help with the funeral.'

'Funeral? They buried him before you got here.'

'Helping with the costs, I mean.' Nash stopped himself. 'I don't need to explain myself to you.'

'Never said you did. But it's strange, though, don't you think? Why you've been here for so long?'

'I grew up around here, felt like spending some time in the old place.'

'I could almost believe that if you weren't staying here with Mich.'

'We're seeing each other now.'

Pete slapped his thigh and laughed. 'You're a good liar, Nash. But from one pro to another, you're not that good. *Seeing each other*, you know that's the funniest thing I've heard in ages.' Pete stopped smiling, a hint of menace in his voice as he said, 'You haven't seen Mich for years. She was whoring the last I heard, and suddenly she's shacked up with you, and you're friends with that kid, too, the one who found Bowen's body, all of you playing happy families. Strange how you disappeared after you visited the bank.' Pete licked his lips. 'This smells like a job to me.'

Nash stood up. 'Sorry to disappoint you, but unfortunately the job only exists in your imagination.'

Pete tapped his nose. 'I can smell it, Nash. Feel it in my water. Things are quiet at the moment. Come on, Nash, please. Just give me a little piece.'

Nash studied him for a moment. 'Do you still carry that little snub nose around with you, Pete?'

Pete nodded. 'Yes, I do.' He slipped a flick knife out of his pocket. 'But I prefer this these days. It's a lot quieter.'

'Makes sense, especially for a man who lives as closely to the edge as you do. You never know when you're going to need it.'

'You trying to threaten me, Nash?'

'No, just giving you a bit of advice that's all.'

Pete laughed. 'You don't frighten me, Nash. Any illusions I ever had about you died after all that stuff with Hilditch. You should save your threats for that little buddy of yours.'

'You keep Jay out of this.'

'So that's his name.' Pete licked his bottom lip. 'Good-looking kid, don't you think?'

Nash pressed the nail of his thumb into the tip of his index finger, pressing harder until the pain proved too much. He shook his head, sighed, then walked away.

'I can help you,' Pete called after him. 'With you and me working together, any scam you've got going would be a helluva lot smoother.'

Nash stopped and turned around. 'You've got it all wrong, Pete. Nothing's going on. If you've got any sense, you'll go back down south.'

Pete shook his head and grinned. 'Nah, there's no rush. It's been ages since I had a break. I might as well enjoy the rest of my holiday. I've paid the B&B for the whole week, extend it if I need to.'

WHEN NASH GOT BACK, he took Mich for a spin in his car. He told her what Pete said and after a long silence, Mich asked him what they should do.

'We need to stay calm,' Nash said. 'Pete's fishing at the moment, trying to wind everyone up. He's no fool, mind, but he still isn't sure what's going on.'

'He seems to have a pretty good idea, if you ask me. I never thought he was that bright.'

'You'd be surprised. If Pete fed on shit, he'd be on a cowpat before even the flies got a whiff.'

Nash drove towards the tops, then took a left to the

Friary. He pulled into the Friary car park, thinking how quiet it was. He glanced around. 'It's bad luck, that's all. It was him that first told me about Bowen. He was sniffing around then. I suppose I was too rattled at the time. I should have taken more notice. He was probably spying on me when I went to the bank. You know what leeches are like.'

Mich pushed back her hair then smoothed her hands down her neck, clasping them together before resting them on her lap. 'You need to get rid of leeches before they suck all the blood from you.' She checked herself in the rearview mirror, smiled approvingly. 'I'll get Shane to have a word with him.'

'Are you stupid or something? That'll make Pete even worse. He'll be on the phone like a shot, attracting all kinds of scum, and they'll come too, offering him their protection and wanting a cut. Pete might be small, but I'm sure he could handle Shane.'

Mich sighed. 'Well, Professor, what do *you* suggest we do?'

Nash ignored the dig. 'We keep calm, for one. We're almost done. Let's not ruin everything now. We don't give Pete a thing. Don't react to any of his little jibes. He'll get bored soon enough.'

'What makes you so sure?'

'Pete likes a quick fix. That's why he's always broke. He's bluffing when he says he's happy to wait. He's never been able to play the long game.'

They got out of the car and walked across the parched brown lawn towards the east wing. Nash stopped for a moment and stared at the grey stone walls and supporting buttresses, then glanced up at the slate roof and the rusty weathervane at the top of the turret. He sensed Mich standing beside him. 'I used to spend hours up here as a kid. I love these old buildings. It's beautiful, don't you think?'

Mich sighed. 'No, I don't. Actually, it gives me the creeps.'

Nash was still angry but ignored her and headed for the path that lay next to the gable end. He stepped through the stone archway, relishing the shade as the track's gradual incline twisted through the ivy-clad trees. He heard Mich behind him, so he waited until she caught up. They ambled on, Mich keeping silent until they reached the first wayside shrine. It stood just over six feet. Nash remembered it being taller. He pushed open its rusty iron gate and nodded at the mosaic on the wall. It was a depiction of Christ walking in the garden of Gethsemane. Nash studied it for a moment, then looked over his shoulder as Mich said, 'What the hell is this place?'

He turned to face her. 'One of the stations of the cross, you know, Calvary.'

She looked at him blankly.

'You're kidding me, right?'

She shook her head.

'I thought you were Catholic?'

Mich rolled her eyes. 'My parents were. I've never said I was.'

Nash sighed. 'But you must have seen places like this before, churches, and shrines, paintings illustrating the last stages of Christ's life?'

Mich smiled. 'What do you think? Do I seem like the religious type?' She stepped closer to the shrine and pulled a face. 'Waste of time, if you ask me.'

Nash breathed deeply. 'It's not a waste of time, Mich. It's art. Except for drinking and screwing around, are you interested in anything?'

'Aww, what's the matter, is little Nash upset? Did these paintings remind him how the teacher used to fiddle about with him in Sunday school?'

Nash gripped her arm. 'Shut it. Don't go too far now.'

She pulled away from him. 'Whoa. I was only kidding. Where the hell did that come from? I know Pete's pissed you off, but don't take it out on me.'

'I'm not taking it out on you. We had words before all this. You need to stop messing about and start acting like a pro.'

'Don't start lecturing me again. You've made your point.'

'Have I? The way you mentioned Shane before, apparently it hasn't sunk in.'

Mich glared at him. 'What's got into you? You can change just like that,' she said, then snapped her fingers and stormed off up the path. Nash followed her, slowing down whenever he got too close.

It took them twenty minutes to reach the top, the heat and the steepness of the hill getting the better of them. It was almost evening now, the sun sinking into the horizon, its orange glow mirrored on the metallic crucifix towering over them. Nash stared up at the emaciated figure of Christ, the bloodied thorn of crowns, and those raised, cerulean blue eyes.

'What are you doing, Nash?' Mich said. 'Thinking of asking him for forgiveness.'

'Perhaps. He's known for welcoming all kinds of trash. Even scum like you and me.'

'I never took you for the religious type.'

'I am, and I'm not.'

'What's that supposed to mean?'

Nash turned to face her. 'I've been a reluctant Christian

all my life. They fill your head with it from the start, in school, the army, TV. There's no getting away from it.'

'I guess so, but I hate religious types. They're the worst kind. They've always got the most to hide.'

'I wouldn't disagree. But we're all fellow passengers to the grave, so we'll be asking for God's forgiveness sooner or later.'

'Not me. No way. I'll be defiant until my last breath.'

Nash flashed her a half smile. 'Let's hope that's the case, huh.'

'Oh, it will be, have no fear of that. It's you I'm worried about.'

Nash frowned and headed back down the path, stopping when Mich blocked his way. 'I'm serious, Nash. You're going soft on me.'

Nash slipped his hand into the top pocket of his shirt and took out his pack of cigarettes. 'Why's that?'

Mich snatched the packet from his hand and took out two cigarettes. She tossed one to Nash, and put the other one in her mouth, puffing on it gently as Nash gave her a light. She took the cigarette out of her mouth. 'All this talk about religion, your reluctance to deal with Pete, Jay, and all the shit you take from Shane.'

Nash smiled to himself. 'Stop trying to wind me up. You know why I'm doing all this.'

'Yeah, I guess. But things have changed so quickly.' She studied him for a moment. 'Don't take this the wrong way, but perhaps we need a fresh approach.'

'I've told you what we need to do. Haven't you been listening?'

Mich took a slow drag of her cigarette. 'Yes, but I'm still entitled to my opinion.'

Nash sighed. 'I never said you weren't. But it's my opinion that counts. We do it my way.'

'But what if your way isn't working?' Her tone softened. There was a kindness in her eyes, and Nash remembered why men were so easily taken in by her. 'We need to move fast, Nash, before things get out of hand. Let's just get your money and leave before it all gets ugly.'

'And how do you suggest we do that?'

'Get Shane to have a word with Jay. The boy's scared of him. Let Shane shake him up a bit. He'll tell us where the money is in no time.'

Nash grabbed her arm. 'I'm warning you. I hope you have said nothing to Shane.'

Mich pulled away. 'No. No. He doesn't have a clue.'

'And what does that tell you?'

'Okay, so he's not that bright—'

Nash laughed. 'Not that bright? He's an idiot. You knew Jay found my money that very first night when Shane told you about him finding a twenty in the woods.'

'I guess you're right.'

'Trust me, I am, and apart from being an idiot, Shane doesn't have an eye for detail. I only work with pros. He'd always be on the brink of messing things up. I've worked with so-called hard men like him before.'

'Like Hilditch you mean?'

He gave her a dirty look, took a drag of his cigarette and started down the path, Mich walking alongside him. They didn't speak for at least five minutes until Nash said, 'You keep working that boyfriend of yours. Renee knows something's going on, and it's paying dividends to keep her like this. The more vulnerable she becomes, the more Jay confides in me. He nearly told me about the money today.

He's going to tell me soon. I'm sure of it, and the moment he does, I can assure you, we'll be gone.'

'You're a heartless bastard.'

He flashed her an exaggerated look of confusion. 'Make your mind up, woman, just now you were accusing me of going soft.'

'All right, I take it back. Well, kind of.'

'What do you mean *kind of*?'

'You've got a soft spot for Jay.'

'What makes you say that?'

'Just the way you are with him.'

'I've got a soft spot for my money. Don't get confused between the two.' He looked into her eyes and smiled. 'And let's not have this conversation about Shane again. Just do as you're told. Or I'll show you how soft I am when I chat with Benny Bray.'

THESE LAST TWO DAYS, Pete was unavoidable. The little runt wore you down. He was tiresome like the heat and as persistent as this summer's stink. His every word grated on Nash's nerves. That wheezy laugh of his was unrelenting. His presence was like an unreachable itch at the roof of your mouth. Nash tried hard to ignore him, which was difficult considering he wasn't at his best. He'd tried reining Mich in, and although she said she understood, he could still see the defiant look in her eyes, but it was Jay who bothered him the most.

As Nash lay on his bed, he kept trying to get the kid's face out of his mind, telling himself he was being stupid. He was going soft in his old age. He'd been out of the *real* game for too long now, and it was showing. Try as he might, Nash

couldn't stop feeling sorry for Jay. With a pill-popping, self-
obsessed mother, an AWOL father replaced by a string of
bullshitting, abusive boyfriends, Jay's future didn't look
bright. The boy had guts, and stamina, too. Something about
him was different. Even from their first encounter, Jay
reminded Nash of himself. Lately, it was more noticeable,
especially now they were spending more time together.
Nash kept telling Jay they were friends and, to be fair, among
all these lies and deceit it was the only thing that was true.

Maybe Nash needed to speak with Jay again, come clean
and tell the boy the truth. With Pete sniffing around and
Mich becoming more unpredictable, what else could he do?
Bowen would have done things differently. He would have
confronted Jay from the start. Even with an element of
doubt, Bowen would have scared the kid into saying
anything, regardless of the consequences. Nash released a
deep sigh and cast such thoughts aside. He had enough
problems with the living. Why make things worse by
thinking about the dead?

LATER THAT EVENING, to make Pete's presence more tolera-
ble, Nash suggested they go out for a drink. It was clear by
the look on Jameson's face that he didn't like that. He kept
dropping hints they should stay in with him, even said he'd
cut his prices; Nash was having none of it. That sticky B&B
bar was too claustrophobic, and he was sick of feeling
confined. He needed a distraction, people, the laughter and
conversation of strangers, anything that would drown out
those niggling doubts inside his head. He needed to subdue
his ghosts and make this holy hell more bearable.

Mich loved going out and did so at every opportunity.
She looked fantastic tonight, her hair blonde and silky,

dressed in a tight, suede frock with lace-up platform sandals to match. Nash couldn't help but smile as they walked into the Pig and Whistle. Mich was like a film star attending the shittiest party. Not that anyone in the pub thought that. It was Saturday night, the music blaring, everyone dressed up to the nines. To them, this was the place of the worldly and the free, a cultural epicentre, bullish and boozy, a place brimming with gossip and laughter.

Nothing else existed outside these nicotine-stained walls. The women were sexy and unforgiving, the men brutal and quick-witted, the savage lash of their tongues unrelenting. This was the place where both young and old could forget, cigarettes and alcohol their lifeblood. Excitement pumped through their veins as they sweated through this endless summer with the tireless certainty that tonight, this one street town was the only place to be.

Nash got the first round, sensing it wouldn't be his last. The first pint was always the best. All the rest just made you bloated. Mich was on the gin. She'd asked for a double, but Nash pretended not to hear her. Pete was drinking bitter with a whiskey chaser. Nash didn't mind that. Pete could handle his drink. The little man was less calculating when he was drunk even though he'd never shut up. But this was the first drink and, for now at least, everyone was behaving themselves.

The jukebox was playing 'Tonight's the Night' and Nash smiled to himself, wondering if it was an omen of things to come.

'Share the joke,' Pete said.

Nash frowned. 'I don't know what you mean.'

Without asking, Pete grabbed Nash's pack of Woodbines, slipped one out, and held it to his mouth. 'Something seems to have amused you.'

Nash flicked open the lid of his gold-coloured Zippo and offered Pete a light. 'It's nothing *you've* said, Pete. You can be sure of that.'

Pete leaned towards the flame, drawing on his cigarette. He took two long drags and then picked up his pint. He gulped down half of it, leaving a moustache of white froth across his top lip. 'So, what is it then?'

Nash tried to ignore him, but he could sense Pete's eyes fix on him. 'You know I can't even remember now.'

Pete took another swig of his pint. 'What if I mention a few things? It might help to jog your memory.'

Nash was about to tell him there was no need but was silenced by a big, clammy hand gripping his shoulder. He didn't need to turn around to know who it was. No, the over-powering smell of *Denim* told him that.

'How's it going, Prof?' Shane said.

'All right,' Nash said. He emptied his glass then stood up. 'What do you want? I'm just about to get another round in.'

'Usual,' Shane said and sat in Nash's chair.

Nash made his way to the bar, weaving through the herd, and took his place in the queue. He could see them from where he stood: Pete smoking his cigarette, Shane sitting close to Mich, his arm resting on the back of her chair, Mich's thigh brushing against his. He wondered where Renee was, but only for a second as his mind filled with thoughts of Jay. He pictured Jay running through the Valley Woods, a low sun behind the trees, the evening silent and full of shadow. A pang of sadness stabbed his guts, and he quickly pushed it away. He felt more certain now. It was time to tell the boy the truth, be firm with him if he had to. It was Nash's money. Why should he feel so bad about it? He'd reward Jay for his trouble, make sure the kid was all right.

When Nash returned with the drinks, Shane didn't move from his seat, and except for Mich moving some empty glasses to one side, nobody offered to help. Nash put the drinks down on the table, then picked up his pint. He took a deep swig, catching Pete's glance as he moved the glass away from his mouth. When he looked at him again, Pete was smirking, a look in his eyes that said, *why don't you make this idiot move?*

'You all right there, Nash?' Pete said. 'You look a bit put out. Don't you want to sit by your fiancée?'

'He's all right,' Shane said and grabbed one of Nash's cigarettes. He stared at Pete as Mich gave him a light, then blew the smoke into his face. 'What is it you do again?'

Pete sat up. 'I never said.'

Shane nodded. 'Yeah, that's why I'm asking you.'

'Oh, you know, a bit of this and that.'

Shane threw Mich a wink, then looked at Pete. 'That's a bit vague, isn't it? What are you a spy or something?'

Pete shook his head. 'No. I'm a fixer. I clear up other people's messes.'

'What, like a cleaner you mean?' Shane said. 'Wiping up all the piss and shit from the Public Lavs and such?'

Pete mumbled something back, his voice drowned out by the roar of Mich's laughter. Pete glared at her, which only encouraged her. He necked down his whiskey. 'No, not really. I help businessmen.'

'*Businessmen*,' Shane said, 'big shot, hey. Anyone I know?'

Pete shook his head. 'I doubt it. Most of my clients are down south.'

Shane rocked back in his chair. 'Try me. I've been around you know.'

'Geoff Lowther? Wally Cummings?' Pete fixed his glare on Mich. 'Benny Bray?'

Shane took a drag of his cigarette. 'Nope, never heard of them.'

Pete flashed a smile. 'You've heard of Benny Bray haven't you, Mich?'

She shook her head, a blank look on her face.

Pete gave her a puzzled look. 'You used to be good friends with him, didn't you?'

Mich opened her mouth to say something, pausing as Nash spoke over her.

'No, she didn't,' Nash said.

Pete kept his eyes on Mich. 'I'm confused now. I thought you and Benny were good friends. Well, that's what retired DI Burris told me.'

'DI Burris?' Shane said.

'Yeah, an old acquaintance,' Pete said. 'He used to work for the CID. He's dead now. He had a heart attack last winter. Shame really, the things he knew was like a little gold mine, but he died before he could cash in.'

'He won't get my sympathy, I hate the pigs,' Shane said before swallowing the dregs of his pint. He slammed down his glass and stood. 'It's my round, I guess.'

'It's Pete's round,' Nash said.

Shane grinned. 'I won't argue with that.' He glanced at Pete. 'I'll have the same as before. I'll come and help you once I've had a slash.'

Shane swaggered over to the gents and Pete slunk off to the bar. Nash was sick of this poisonous little man, loathing the grey hues of his skin, those deep-set eyes, and the oily sheen of his hair.

He sensed Mich staring at him, and when he looked at her, she said, 'What have you told him?'

'Nothing. I swear to it.'

'So where did all that stuff about Benny Bray come from?'

'DI Burris, I guess, because I never said anything.'

Mich took out a cigarette. 'What are we going to do about it?'

'We're leaving.'

'When?'

'Sometime tomorrow, after I get the truth out of Jay.'

Mich smiled. 'And how do you plan to do that?'

'I'll take him for a walk, talk to him, man to man.'

'And what am I supposed to do?'

'Wait for me here, if you like.'

'I said I'd meet Shane in the morning.'

'Still do that. It'll be good to have lover boy out of the way.'

Mich lit her cigarette, still staring at him as she took a deep drag. She exhaled the smoke. 'How can I be sure you won't leave without me?'

Nash shrugged. 'Trust? Or take my car if you like.'

'I might do that. But either way, I need to know every detail. What time you're going to see him. Where you'll be.'

'Sure, you can know everything as long as you do what I say.'

PART III

TAKE THE MONEY AND RUN

1

KISS AND SAY GOODBYE

A s she drove to the ferry, Mich turned the day's events over in her mind. It all seemed unreal, like a distant nightmare.

She started the day as planned, intending to do everything Nash told her. She was washed and dressed before seven-thirty a.m., and even took an early breakfast. She could never stomach Jameson's daily offering of grease, black bits, and burnt sausages, so settled for her usual: one slice of dry toast and a cup of warm tea. She sat facing the patio doors that opened out onto the back. She loathed the silence, these quiet hours of the morning. She could see the estuary from where she sat. The sun's red eye bled across the water as it loitered above the shore. She sighed at the heat; this endless summer wasn't the only thing that had outstayed its welcome. At least this was her last day in this godforsaken place. She smiled at that, and the thought of leaving comforted her.

Mich pushed back her chair and stood, trying to hide her surprise as she saw Pete standing in the doorway. He was wearing a pair of taupe linen slacks and a white cotton shirt three sizes too big. His hair was slathered with Bryl-creem and the skin on his sunburnt face had peeled. Having watched him these last couple of days, Mich wondered how he stayed so slim. This irksome, emaciated little man seemed to be always eating and drinking. Even now, as he stared at her with those sunken eyes, he was chewing something. Mich never liked Pete. She didn't trust him. She gave him one of her looks. A look that both expressed her disgust and questioned what he was doing there.

She walked towards him, stopping as he blocked her way.

'What do you want?' she said, as though he were a bothersome child. 'Come on, Pete, spit it out. I've got things to do.'

He flashed her a nicotine-stained smile. 'No need to be like that. I only want to talk with you.'

'I'm busy. It'll have to wait.'

She tried to squeeze past him, but Pete stood his ground. 'I think you'll want to hear this.'

'What makes you so sure?'

'By the look on your face last night when I mentioned Benny Bray.'

She felt her heart pounding against her chest and, as though the blood had suddenly drained from her, her legs felt weak. 'Benny Bray? Why would I be interested in him?'

'You know why.'

Mich smiled. 'I've no idea what you're talking about.'

Pete nodded and moved aside.

She caught a waft of his smell as she brushed past him, a sickening mix of sweat, cigarettes, and cheap aftershave.

'Are you sure you know nothing about it?' Pete said.

Mich stopped then turned to face him. 'I already said so, didn't I?'

'I'd like you to think about it again, mull it over for a few seconds before I make a phone call.'

'To whom?'

Pete grinned. 'Benny Bray. I need to tell him I bumped into an old friend of his. Only the thing is, she's not as friendly as he might think.'

MICH AGREED to talk about it on her way to Shane's. She wanted to take Nash's TR6, but Pete refused and insisted on driving her there himself. She gave him directions to the tops, saying nothing else until they were ten minutes into their journey. She wanted to tell him his car stank, but all she did was wind down the window. 'So, Pete, what do you want exactly?'

Pete eased off the gas and fixed his stare on the road. 'You know what I want: a piece of what you and Nash are up to, a little slice of the cake.'

Mich pointed to the sign ahead, considering her answer as Pete took a left at the crossroads.

She looked at him and sighed. 'You keep going on about this.' She turned to face the road. 'And we keep telling you nothing's going on. What makes you so sure there is?'

He didn't answer her immediately. He kept driving, steering the car through the bends, squinting at the light filtering through the dying trees. Then he pulled into a layby, switched off the engine, and stared ahead. He looked different. It was as though something possessed him, and a dark, malicious creature lurked behind those small grey eyes. He slipped his hand into his pocket and pulled out a flick knife. 'Stop pissing me about. *Nothing is going on.*' He raised his voice. 'Bullshit. You and Nash aren't an item, and who's this Shane, acting like he owns the

place. I've never seen Nash let anyone speak to him like
that. Answer me.'

Mich had been in this kind of situation so many times:
angry, ineffectual men threatening her and telling her what
to do. In most cases she played the victim, especially when
she was whoring, it was the only way to make sure she got
paid. She'd only been truly frightened once: the time DI
Burris and his partner pulled her in and beat the crap out of
her. Pete wasn't in their league. He was only dangerous
because of the things he potentially knew.

'You tell me something first,' she said.

'Go on.'

'What do you think you know about Benny Bray
and me?'

'You know what.'

She forced a smile. 'No, I don't. Otherwise, I wouldn't be
asking.'

Pete flicked open his knife and smoothed it across the
top of his hand. He gave her that sickly grin of his. 'I know
you grassed him up. Burris let it slip one night when he was
drunk.'

'What did he say?'

'Enough for me to know he was telling the truth.'

Mich lowered her eyes. 'If that's true, then why didn't
Burris use that information himself?'

'Who says he wasn't going to? Perhaps, like me, he was
saving it for a rainy day.'

She glanced out the window. 'Have you seen the weather
lately? It hasn't rained for a while.'

Pete sniffed the air. 'Oh, I guarantee you it's about to. I
can smell it. In fact, once Benny Bray gets to hear about you,
there's going to be quite a storm.'

She turned towards him. 'Fine. Do your worst. Call him. I'll be gone before he gets here. I'll take my chances.'

She watched the certainty drain from his eyes. Saw it replaced by shock. A different man stared back at her. A man who, moments ago, held all the cards. A man with a look of fearful desperation as the other player called his bluff and showed him a better hand.

Mich gave him an indignant smile. 'What's wrong, Pete? You've gone quiet all of a sudden?'

He flashed the knife in front of her then grabbed her face with his free hand. 'You whore. You stinking whore. You tell me what's going on before things get nasty.'

She felt the spittle on her face, unable to decide whether the smell was from Pete's breath or his fingers.

'Please, Pete,' she said, 'please don't hurt me.' And as the knife loosened in Pete's hand, she grabbed his testicles, squeezing them hard as he cried out, then snatched the knife from his hand.

Years of abuse taught her to be quick. It urged her on, enticing her to slash the knife across Pete's leg, forcing her to scream and cry as she stabbed the blade repeatedly into his throat.

Tears coursed down her cheeks.

Snot bubbled from her nose and dribbled into her mouth. But she didn't care. All that mattered was that she was free of him. Not this ferret-like little man. But the threat that plagued her days: her fear of Benny Bray.

When it was over, she pushed Pete's lifeless body away from her, suddenly conscious of the heat and the arid smell of the earth.

But it was the silence that struck her most, as though this hellish land watched her with bated breath.

.   .   .

SHE DROVE Pete's car onto a dirt track that led into the woods. Thinking how light he was as she dragged his body through the dead grass and lifted it into the boot.

She picked up Pete's snub nose from the ground, holding the pistol tight as she stood staring into the trees.

So many things surprised her: how calm she was and how easy it was to kill. She used her blouse to wipe up most of the blood, concealing the rest with a blanket and a few rags she found in the boot. She also found one of Pete's old shirts, trying not to retch as she changed into it. Once she was done, she sat in the driver's seat. She needed tears now, something more than words to convince Shane. She closed her eyes, thinking about all the vile things that had happened to her throughout her life. She pictured her Uncle Marty, slobbering all over her, her junky mother burning her arms with cigarettes, and that chain of boys from her old school.

She thought of all the men who pleasured themselves inside her, slapped her, beaten, and threatened her, used her, treated her like some cheap thing. She let the rage swell inside her, bulging like a blister, sobbing the moment it burst. Then she drove out of the woods and headed towards Shane's, holding onto those tears, needing them more than ever now, relishing them for so many reasons.

WHEN SHE ARRIVED at the old bungalow, Shane was waiting outside. He cast the car a suspicious glance, rushing towards it the moment he saw her face.

He swung open the driver's door. 'Jesus, Mich, what's wrong? You've got blood on your face. What the hell's happened to you?'

'It's Nash's blood. I told him about *us*. He went crazy.'

She let him take her hand and guide her out of the car. They looked at each other in silence for a second until she pushed her face into his chest, sobbing as she said, 'What are we going to do?'

He rubbed her back, trying to soothe her. 'Leave everything to me. We'll be okay. This is what we want, right?'

She nodded, causing him to hold her tighter.

'I'll go and sort Professor out soon, and Renee, too. From now on, it's just you and me.'

She stepped back and fixed her eyes on his. 'I don't think it's going to be that easy.'

Shane frowned. 'Why?'

She sighed. 'It's...it's kind of complicated.'

He seemed puzzled, as though any potential difficulties were beyond his comprehension. Mich almost laughed at the stupid look on his face but maintained the act, there was too much at stake now.

She told him everything, her version of it at least.

At first, Shane didn't appear to care that Mich, and Nash were running a con. He seemed angry with himself, but more so with Jay. 'The little bastard. The thieving little bastard, hiding that money all this time, making a fool out of—' He gave her a sharp look. 'I suppose that's what you were doing as well?'

'That's what I came here for. Until I met you. Until I fell in love.'

He glanced down at the ground, trying to conceal his smile, as though these were the words he'd been waiting for. He raised his head and looked at her. 'And how do I know that's true?'

'I'm here, aren't I? I could have played along with it. But I didn't want to hurt you. I'm taking an enormous risk telling you all this.'

He nodded at the car. 'And where did you get this?'

'It's Pete's. I just needed to get out of there. He just gave me his keys, lent me one of his shirts. He saw how upset I was, didn't argue.'

Shane raised his eyes and sighed. 'So, what now?'

'We need to find them. Jay and Nash are probably down by the estuary as we speak. Then we need to follow them and demand our share of the cash. God knows what Nash is planning on doing with it now.'

Shane nodded. 'You leave him to me.'

'Don't mess with him, Shane, especially now.'

'What do you mean don't mess with *him*? I'll rip his head off. The prick's scared of his own shadow.'

Mich shook her head and sighed, then nodded at Shane's van. 'You drive.'

'What about Pete's car?'

She studied him for a second. 'Oh... I'll call him later, tell him where it is. He can come and fetch it himself. I'm too shaken up to drive now.'

She walked to the car, opened the driver's door, and grabbed her handbag from the seat. Holding the handbag close to her chest, she turned around, then gave Shane a look that said, *what are you waiting for?*

He nodded at Pete's car. 'I need to move that around to the back. It's blocking my van.'

She gripped the keys. 'I'll do it. Then let's get a move on.'

MICH KEPT TELLING Shane to slow down. The last thing they needed was the police pulling them over. Not that there was any sign of them, but she couldn't afford to take chances. Shane did as he was told, sighing with impatience whenever they stopped at a junction or a set of lights. He kept tapping his finger against the steering wheel, its sound accentuated by the dead silence.

Mich grew to hate Sunday mornings here. The place was dead enough in the week but on Sundays it was lifeless. There were few cars on the road and every house they passed looked abandoned. She watched a trail of birds flying towards the sea. Her stomach churned at the sight of them, her anticipation growing at the thought that soon she would escape, too.

It didn't take them long to get to the estuary and, on Mich's instruction, Shane parked near the old docks.

'What now?' he said. 'I can go looking for them, give Nash a slap, force that little tyke to tell us where the money is. All I—'

'Shush.'

He glowered at her, opened his mouth to say something but paused as she pointed at two figures, a man, and a boy, sitting on the rocks. Nash and Jay, looking out across the water. Nash had his arm around Jay's shoulder, the boy occasionally nodding as Nash gestured with his free hand. They looked like father and son, the best of friends.

As she watched them in silence, Mich wondered what Nash was telling the boy. Not that she needed to guess. No, she was all too aware of Nash's sugar-coated words. She'd been manipulated by them for so long. He'd probably started the conversation with something light, talking about the TV programs Jay loved, putting the kid at ease with that soft, casual tone of his. Then, gradually, he'd change the subject, talking about friendship, loyalty, and trust. He'd weave in little bits about himself: how hard things were lately, how broke he was, sad even, growing more desperate. Words designed to pull at the boy's heartstrings and plant those malignant seeds of guilt. Nash was good at that. A master at nurturing culpability and remorse, probably because they were so much a part of him. Jay didn't stand a chance. The poor kid, desperate to tell someone, grateful that it was his best friend, Nash.

Mich tapped Shane's arm as Nash and Jay got up.

'Reverse past those crates. Don't let them see us.'

Shane mumbled something under his breath but did as instructed. He breathed deeply. 'Now what?'

'We follow them.'

'I can't see a thing from here.'

'Wind down the window and listen out for Nash's engine.'

They sat quietly. Each second felt like hours, and Mich could hear her heart beating inside her chest. She half expected Nash to suddenly appear in front of the window, or Shane to shout or do something equally unpredictable. She swallowed against the dryness of her mouth. The air, a clammy mix of silt and mud, was so strong she could taste it. She wiped the sweat from her palms. Then she heard an engine and waited with bated breath until Nash's car drove down the old Dock Road before ordering Shane to follow.

They kept a safe distance, following Nash's car along the coast road then left up the Well Hill. She wouldn't miss anything about this place, the estuary's ghostly morning mist, the valley's stench of wild garlic, and that unforgiving stare from the marble statue of Christ. He was looking down at them now as they reached the brow of the hill, holding out his welcoming hands, that kind smile of his fooling no one.

Jesus had never been there for Mich, and she was confident he wouldn't be there for her now.

She fixed her eyes on the road. What did she care? In a few hours, she wouldn't need anyone. She smiled momentarily, sensing that this time tomorrow she'd be able to look after herself. Yet the feeling was short-lived, suddenly realising, as they turned left onto Whitford Street, there was no sign of Nash's car.

Shane banged the steering wheel with his fist. 'Jesus, I knew we should have driven faster.'

'Put your foot down then.'

'I am for Christ's sake. Which way?'

'I don't know, keep following the road, I guess.'

'What if he hasn't gone this way?'

'We'll turn around then, won't we. We're bound to catch up with him sooner or later.'

Shane pressed harder on the gas, gaining speed, driving sixty in a thirty zone. He caught up to the other cars, frantically beeping his horn, shouting for them to pull over. None of them budged, so he overtook a line of traffic the moment he saw a gap.

'Jesus, Shane, slow down. I said to hurry, not get us both killed.'

He took a sharp left, turned the van around, and headed back towards town.

'What are you doing?' Mich said,

He flashed her an angry look. 'I'm going to try the Bron Park Road. He must have gone that way. Otherwise, we would have caught him up by now, and stop shouting.'

Mich closed her eyes for a second. She felt gutted. As though all her hopes and dreams had been snatched away from her. She raked her fingers through her hair, wanting to pull it out from the roots. Then she saw it. 'There,' she shouted, pointing at Nash's car parked on the opposite side of the road. She scanned the area. 'Where do you think he is?'

Shane pulled over and turned off the engine. 'The footpath he's parked by leads to Bron Woods. That's where Jay found that dead guy.'

'Bowen.'

Shane nodded, then smiled. 'The little shit probably kept it hidden where he found it.' He reached for the door handle, pausing as Mich grabbed his arm.

'Let's take it slowly, huh? Creep up on them.'

Shane opened the door and stood outside. She watched him for a second, grabbed her handbag, then did the same. He mumbled something as he locked the van but Mich didn't answer, feeling the sweat run down her back as she crossed the road.

Shane led her up the footpath, guiding her slowly through the overgrown weeds, pointing out the dense clumps of ivy and whispering, 'Mind you don't trip.'

A rank smell tainted the air: parched earth and infected leaves. *Jesus,* Mich thought, *it smells like something died here.* She breathed through her mouth, each blast of stale air settling on her throat. It was quieter; the noise of the passing traffic faded into the distance. All Mich heard now was the snap beneath her feet and the heaviness of her breath.

As they reached a clearing in the woods, Shane motioned for her to stop. She stared at the big, dilapidated house, thinking how she'd seen nothing quite like it. The woods had claimed it. Ivy twisted through every opening and crack, climbing the walls, smothering the window frames and the open rafters. Wild grass covered the lower floor, the place a synthesis of the natural and the man-made, congruent, as though it had been constructed among the trees.

Shane looked back at her over his shoulder. 'They're at the back of the house,' he whispered. 'You grab Jay, leave the

Professor to me.' She gave him a look that warned him to be careful, but he ignored it.

They crept through the grass, and she could hear Nash talking now, the softness of his voice carried by the dead silence.

Jay reminded her of a startled rabbit as he caught sight of them. The boy stared with his mouth wide open, motionless. Nash remained calm, casual even, his shirt sleeves rolled up, his hands covered with soil. He glanced down at the briefcase at his feet, looked at Mich and said, 'I told you not to involve him. You just won't listen, will you? I thought we had an understanding.'

Mich opened her mouth to say something, but Shane spoke over her.

'Oh, we've got an understanding all right. The thing is, Professor, it seems like you and this little shit here are cut from the same cloth. You both like to tell porkies.'

Shane glared at the boy. 'Get home, Jay. Get home, I said. Come on. Now. Home. Do as I say, or it'll make things worse for you later.'

Nash held out his hand. 'Come and stand by me, Jay. He won't hurt you.'

Jay shuffled closer to Nash and stood by his side. He clenched his fists, a defiant look in his eyes.

Nash rested a hand on Jay's shoulder. 'Good lad. Friends need to stick together, especially now we're partners.'

Mich sighed. 'Don't listen to him, Jay. He isn't your friend. He's just using you.' She nodded down at the briefcase. 'To get his hands on that.'

'He explained everything,' Jay said. 'He's going to give Mam and me half of it. Help us buy a big house.'

Mich laughed. 'Sure, he is. But even if that was true, he

doesn't have it to give, because half of that money belongs to me.'

Nash removed his hand from Jay's shoulder. 'That contract's void now, Mich. It ended the moment you turned against me.'

'It's not like that, Nash. I'll explain it to you later.'

Nash shook his head. 'There's no need. You've made your choices. You and I are through.'

Mich glared at him. 'Bastard. I want my share. Now. I've earned it.'

'You've earned my silence,' Nash said, 'and nothing more. Don't worry; I won't tell Benny Bray. I think you've got a bargain. Don't you?'

Mich slipped her hand into her handbag, pausing as Shane stood in front of her. 'Watch your mouth, Prof. She's taking her share, all right? And the way you're acting, we might even take all of it.'

Nash took a deep breath. 'Why are you still here, Shane? I don't want to see you anymore.' He clapped his hands. 'Go on, scram. None of this has anything to do with you.'

Shane appeared shocked at first. But it only lasted a few seconds. That semi-permanent mean look on his face rapidly returning, holding him steadfast as he launched himself at Nash.

It was over quicker than it began. Shane threw a punch. Nash ducked, turned on a sixpence, and pressed his back into Shane's chest. Then he rammed his elbow into Shane's face, causing Shane to lean forward and cover his bloody nose with his hands. Nash slipped behind him, grabbed the tail of Shane's shirt, and delivered a swift, hard kick in the nuts, sending him face first onto the ground.

Nash threw Jay a wink. 'The thing you need to know about guys like Shane, Jay, is that they know how to pick their fights, they build a reputation on it. I blame his mother. She probably spoiled him rotten.' Nash stamped on the back of Shane's head. 'This prick grew up without people telling him *No*. He does all right in a small town. But he's scared to do anything else.'

Nash kicked Shane in the stomach, motioned to do it again until Mich shouted, 'All right, Nash. You've made your point. That's enough now.'

She pointed the pistol at him. Her legs were like jelly and her hand wouldn't stop shaking. She felt breathless, her heart thumping, faster and faster, as though it was about to burst from her chest.

Nash slowly held up his hands. 'Simmer down, Mich. The show's over.' He glanced down at Shane. 'You have to admit it, though, this prick had it coming for ages.'

'I want my money, Nash.'

'You can have some of it.' He nodded at the pistol. 'Where the hell did you get that, anyway?'

'There's a lot you don't know about me.' She straightened her arm and gripped the pistol tighter. 'A few grand's no good. I want at least half of it.'

'I can't do that, Mich. Now drop that thing, before I do something both of us will regret.'

Looking back at it now, lowering the pistol and handing it to Nash was probably the wisest thing she could have done. But she wasn't trying to be wise at the time. She just wanted her money and for Nash to stop giving her orders. So many thoughts flashed through her mind: how vulnerable she felt, tired, sick of men like Pete, Benny Bray, and Nash. They were always wanting control, always telling her what to do. Nash wasn't as bad as most of them. But he was just as weak, never letting go, always hanging onto a good thing. No matter what he promised, Mich knew she'd never be free of him. He'd always use what he knew about her, keeping it as insurance, probably until his dying day. She couldn't live like that. No, not anymore. When good fortune stares you in the face, a girl must take her chances.

Mich squeezed the trigger and watched as Nash fell, her ears deafened by a crack of thunder.

TRY AS SHE MIGHT, sitting in the ferry bar, a gin and tonic in her hand, Mich couldn't stop picturing their faces. Jay stayed silent throughout, pale, shaking, obeying Mich's every word. Initially, Shane looked shocked. He kept shaking his head in disbelief, glancing between Nash's body and the blood on his hands, as though unable to decide what bewildered him more, Nash getting shot, or how easily Nash beat him up.

Shane also followed Mich's every command, setting about his task as though he were in a daze. He dragged Nash's body to the back of the house, buried it in a shallow grave, then covered it with brambles and leaves. When he was done, Mich handed him some cash. 'There's almost ten grand there,' she said. 'It should see you right for a while.'

He stared at the bundle of notes, looked at her and said, 'And that's it?'

'What else did you expect?'

'What about us?'

'There never was an *us*. You were just too stupid to see that.'

'You bitch. I could just go and tell the pigs you know, right now.'

'You could, but you won't. You're as much a part of this as I am. You've just hidden his body, remember. What do they call it, guilty by association?'

'What if somebody finds him?'

Mich glanced at the house. 'Nash checked us out of the B&B this morning. The owner thinks we've left. No one's looking for us. It could be years before anyone finds his body. A few months, at least.'

'And we're just supposed to leave him like that?'

She pointed at the wads of notes. 'I think that will ease your conscience and don't go spending it too soon. Stay in that shack of yours for a while. I'd keep a low profile if I were you.'

Shane nodded at Jay. 'What about him?'

'He won't say anything.' Mich gave Jay a sad smile. 'Sorry love, but you're not my problem. Make things easy for yourself and do as Shane says.'

Shane stuffed the money into his pockets then gave Jay a shove. 'Perhaps I don't need him. I could just wring his scrawny neck.'

Mich shook her head. 'No, you haven't got it in you. But I wouldn't advise that. He's your only insurance.'

As always, Shane looked confused. 'How do you work that out?'

'He's your alibi, stupid. He's the only one who can verify your innocence if the shit ever hits the fan.'

Then she turned her back on them and hurried down the footpath, trying hard to forget that look of fear on Jay's face.

2

MAN IN THE HILLS

For Jay, it felt like the world had ended. The scorched fields lay silent beneath a blood-red sky. The humid, foul air lingered. Swarms of ladybirds infested everything, the first omen of the pestilence to come.

They'd been in that old bungalow for only a few hours, but it already felt like weeks. All Jay could think about was Nash. He pictured him dead among the dry leaves, more so whenever he closed his eyes. So much shocked him. To begin with, there was the revelation about the money, and how Nash knew about it all along. Jay felt only rage at first. But when he looked into Nash's eyes, he realised how sorry he was. His anger quickly turned into forgiveness and all that pent-up guilt into relief. Jay believed every word when Nash told him that he'd see him and his mam right. He also promised to deal with Shane and, for a short while at least, that came true.

At first, Jay thought Shane was going to take the money and run, which would have been better for everyone. But he was too selfish and cowardly to do that, and by the fearful look in his eyes, Jay knew he wasn't even tempted. It didn't stop Jay from trying, though. 'You can have all the money,' he said. 'Just leave. I won't say a thing.'

Shane shook his head. 'No. You're staying with me. Just like Mich said, if this goes tits up, you're my only alibi. You'll tell them I had nothing to do with it. D'you hear me?'

Shane cried like a baby as he told Renee his version of events. Jay could tell he wasn't acting. Shane was scared, like a child running back to his mam, each exaggerated sob filled by genuine fear and sorrow. Shane told Renee how sorry he was. He was ashamed of himself; he didn't know what to do. He told her how he'd fallen for Mich's every word. How manipulative she was. 'I know it takes two, Renee, and God knows I played my part in it. But she was persistent. She wouldn't take no for an answer, and now I know why.'

Shane never mentioned he'd wanted to leave with Mich, and during their drive back home, he warned Jay to do the same. He mentioned the money, though, convincing Renee that he'd demanded his share after threatening to tell the police. Renee was angry to begin with, and it was the first time Jay had seen her shout Shane down. Then she started crying, screaming into Shane's face, threatening to go to the police herself, furious as she pushed him away. Shane begged for her forgiveness. Said he loved her. That without her by his side, life had no purpose. He told her how worried he was. The money would give them a fresh start, but for now, they needed to lie low.

Renee fell for all of it. But that didn't surprise Jay. It was just as Nash had taught him: People believe what they want to believe, especially if they're desperate for it to be true.

Shane was quiet afterwards, getting things sorted, keeping his head down, taking everything they needed to that crappy bungalow. At least he left Jay alone for a while.

In fact, he couldn't look him in the eye. Jay sensed it was shame. They exchanged glances sometimes as though neither of them could quite believe it. Nash was so swift, putting Shane on his arse with the same amount of ease as a giant squatting a fly. Jay loved Nash's every move, the way he spun around, used his elbow instead of his fist, as though knowing exactly what Shane was about to do.

JAY SPENT most of the evening in the back garden, leaning against the fence and gazing into the woods. The stream had run dry, leaving a small valley of parched earth cutting through the surrounding banks. He couldn't bear it inside. The place smelt strange, a mixture of peppermint and mothballs. It was dusty, too, and the longer he stared at those half-papered walls, the more he could see the cracks.

The sound of his mam's voice, constantly reassuring Shane, sickened him.

'Don't blame yourself,' she kept saying. 'You reacted better than most,' calling him 'lover' and 'hon'.

Shane was a coward. Jay knew his mam thought that. He could see the worry in her eyes, and that troubled smile she gave him told him that everything felt wrong. She wanted to go to the police at first, but Shane would have none of it: begging her not to, pleading for her to stand by him between each sob.

JAY SENSED someone standing behind him even before his mam spoke. 'All right?' she said as he turned round. Her hair looked almost golden against the sunlight, and her skin seemed less pale. She'd been off the gin all day, and it was starting to show. A glimpse of light shone in her eyes, growing brighter as time passed. She hadn't cried for hours and stopped feeling sorry for herself, just like his mam of old.

She grabbed his hand and drew him closer. 'What are you up to? You're spending a lot of time out here.'

'Nothing, just hanging around. I was thinking of exploring those woods.'

'Best not, hey. Stay where I can see you. Remember what Shane said, *we need to keep a low profile.*'

Jay frowned. God, she was even talking like him now.

'What's up?' she said.

'Nothing.'

'Yes, there is. I can tell.'

She knew what was wrong. They both did, and Jay could feel himself getting more frustrated as he wondered why she wouldn't admit to it.

'You know, you could have told me about the money,' she said. 'I wouldn't have told anyone. I would have kept it between you and me.' She turned her head sideways, sighing as Shane watched them from the kitchen window. She looked at Jay. 'Then maybe we wouldn't be in this mess.'

Jay was too angry to speak at first. What was she trying to say? That all this was his fault? He clenched his fists and fixed her with a hard stare. 'Are you blaming me for all this?'

'No, love, I'm not. It's just—'

'That money belongs to Nash. Things would have been all right if Mich and that prick hadn't spoiled everything.'

'Shane didn't shoot him, though, did he? I know he's mental sometimes, but he'd never do that.'

'He tried to hurt Nash, though, until Nash gave him a hiding.' There was a thickness in his voice. 'Shane wouldn't even be here if Mich hadn't dumped him.'

'Don't say that, Jay.'

'Why? You know it's true.' He sniffed back a tear. 'Why are you always defending him? Why can't you be on my side for once?'

She hugged him, squeezing tighter. 'I am on your side, love, always was and always will be.'

Jay could have stood like that forever, the sun beating down on him, soothed by the rise and fall of his mam's chest and her warm, perfumed touch.

She let go of him, stepping back as she rested her hands on his shoulders. She wore a serious expression and for once she looked like a grown-up. 'This is a difficult time, Jay. We need to stick together, right?'

He shrugged. 'Why can't it just be you and me?'

She laughed but only for a moment, swallowing it in one quick breath. 'You'd like that, wouldn't you?'

'Why can't it, though?'

'It's complicated.'

'How?'

'People need different kinds of love. You'll understand what I mean when you're older.'

Jay understood all right. There was nothing complicated about it. His mam was needy. Shane was a prick and a bully, dragging them into this mess, telling her what she wanted to hear so he could get his way. But Jay didn't tell her that. Instead, he nodded, holding her hand as they strolled back to the bungalow.

'This is a big chance for all of us,' Renee said. 'We can change our lives. We need to make the most of it. That kind of money never comes to people like us.'

'But that's Nash's money.'

'It was. But he's someplace else now and has no use for it.'

As they reached the front door Jay stopped, causing his

mam to stop too. Those weren't his mam's words. Before she met Shane, she wouldn't have dreamed of talking like that.

'But you said it yourself, Mam. How it was a sin and a shame to leave him like that.'

She bowed her head slightly. 'It is.' She sighed. 'But we've come too far now, love. What do you think would happen if we went to the police?'

Jay shrugged.

'Shane would go down, for one thing. He couldn't go to prison again. It would be the ruin of him. They'd pin everything on him. They'd have me on something as well.' She smoothed her hand down his arm. 'You know what the police are like, probably put you in care, and you can say ta-ra to that money and any chance of a good life.'

There was genuine fear in his mam's voice. But it wasn't the only thing that silenced him. A feeling of dread took root in his stomach, convincing him there was truth in everything she said.

Sunday night's top forty was Jay's favourite program on the radio, and he kept turning up the volume whenever he heard a song he liked. Shane warned him about it a few times. 'Turn it down. I can't hear myself think.'

The comment made Jay smile. *Can't hear myself think.* Who was he trying to kid? Shane could be alone on a desert island and he still wouldn't come up with a good idea. Even if his life depended on it, which, in the current situation, it did.

Shane seemed more relaxed now. That frightened look on his face, which kept him silent for so long, was slowly fading. He was still jumpy, occasionally pacing up and down the hall, or watching from the kitchen window. But there was a hint of something else in his eyes. A weird look. One that seemed to say: *You know what, I just might get away with it.* Shane wasn't a hundred percent sure. Jay knew that. He could tell by the way Shane still wouldn't venture too far from the house, and how he'd made Renee drive into town to get a load of cans and a Chinese takeaway. At first, Renee wanted Jay to accompany her. But Shane begged her to let him stay, giving her some bullshit story about how he didn't want to be left alone. It seemed to convince her. She kissed them both goodbye, told them not to worry if she was late back. She needed to take her time because she wasn't used to driving, especially a van.

Jay didn't enjoy being alone with Shane. He was fidgety, kept sighing, and smoked too many cigarettes. Yet the thing he hated most was the way Shane looked at him. Jay pretended not to notice at first. Then he'd turn his head quickly, catch Shane in full glare, his shark eyes fixed on him. He tried holding Shane's stare with his own, and it worked for a while until the old Shane returned. He was like a man possessed. The poise confident, a dark intention in the eyes as he sat there brooding. He tut-tutted whenever Jay spoke, raised his eyes, and sighed when Jay started singing along to a song.

Jay was persistent, only stopping when Shane said, 'I need to find them and kill them.'

Jay frowned. 'Who?'

'Whoever told you that you could sing.'

'I used to be in the school choir. Mr. Fisher and Mam said I had a wonderful voice.'

'That Fisher's a piss-head and your mam's delusional.'

'She must be,' Jay mumbled.

'What was that?'

'Nothing.'

'It didn't sound like nothing to me. If you're going to say stuff, then you need to have the balls to back it up.'

'Like you, you mean?'

Shane slammed his hands down on the arms of his chair. Then he got up and walked over to Jay. He pushed his face closer, his breath stale, his two-day stubble grazing Jay's skin. 'There you go again,' he said in a low voice, 'mouthing off, passing little comments without saying what you mean.'

Jay kept silent, staring at the dark shadows around Shane's eyes, and the traces of brown in the iris, which reminded him of tiny spirals of blood floating in a cold, green pool.

Shane sighed. 'What were you talking about?'

'When?'

'Just then, dickhead.'

Jay shrugged. 'I don't know... I... I...'

'I–I, listen to yourself. Spit it out, you stammering little shit.'

'You said I haven't got the balls, but you're the one who's frightened.'

Shane grabbed Jay's arms and forced him to stand. 'You cheeky little bastard. I'll show you what it means to be scared.' He dragged Jay into the hall. Jay tried to pull away, but Shane was too strong, tightening his grip as he swung the front door open. He pushed Jay outside and shoved him across the grass. The air was warm, the evening sky caught between light and darkness. It felt as though the night was waiting for something: Thin drifts of cloud loitered above the trees. A faint smell of smoke lingered in the muggy air.

Jay listened to the dead grass snap beneath his feet, wincing whenever Shane's sweaty palm pressed into his back. He'd no idea what Shane was planning. All he knew was that they were walking towards the woods, and he grew more nervous with each step.

'Can we go back now, Shane?'

'Later, after we've played a game.'

'What game?'

'A game to see who gets more frightened.'

Jay made a run for it, stopping momentarily at the sound of a car. Both stood still, watching the bright glow of headlights sweep through the trees. Jay pulled free from Shane's grip and ran to the van driving towards them. Renee smiled at him at first then the look on her face turned serious. He chased after the van as she pulled into the driveway.

Renee stepped out of the van with a panicked look on her face. 'What's happened, Jay? What's wrong?'

'Nothing,' Shane said before Jay could answer.

She slammed the van door. 'Doesn't seem like nothing to me, and what were you doing over there?'

'Going for a walk,' Shane said. 'It's stifling in that bungalow, wanted to get some air, have a bit of fun.'

Renee turned to Jay. 'You all right, love?'

Jay nodded.

'Okay.' She handed him the keys. 'Start getting the shopping and those cans out of the van; then we'll have our takeaway.' She gave him a wink. 'I got you some spareribs.'

Jay took to his task without protest, trying not to look at Shane as his mam helped him carry the shopping into the house.

Shane didn't do a thing. He just grabbed a can, flipped it open, then leaned against the car and watched. When Jay came back outside, there was a cocksure glint in Shane's eyes. He wore that familiar indignant half smile. The look of a man who'd left his worries behind and was set to spend the night drinking.

You think you're clever, don't you? Jay thought. *We'll see who gets frightened later. I'll teach you.*

JAY ATE his food in silence, relishing each chip soaked in salt and vinegar, each scoop of fried rice slathered in sweet 'n sour sauce. Shane wouldn't shut up. He kept talking with his mouthful, asking Renee the same questions. 'Are you sure now? Did everything seem all right?'

Renee sighed. 'Yes. How many times do I need to tell you?'

Shane sucked the curry sauce from his fingers. 'As many times as it takes. Come on, Renee, you can't blame me for asking.' He took a swig of lager. 'Tell me again. Who did you see?'

Renee rested her plate on her lap then wiped her hands with a paper towel. 'The women in the offy, the till girl in Tesco's, and Edna next door when I popped in for a few knick-knacks.'

Shane pointed at her with a chip. 'And she seemed all right to you?'

'She seemed fine. Just asked if we were enjoying our time at the bungalow.'

Shane swallowed his food. 'You told her we were going?'

'What else was I supposed to say? She's got eyes like a hawk that one, a nosy beak, too. There's no point lying to her. She'd sense something was wrong straight away.'

Shane thought about that for a moment then nodded in agreement. 'And she mentioned nothing, local gossip, if anything had been in the papers?'

'Nope. I asked her what's new, and she said not a thing. Trust me, she would have mentioned it if anything was going on. Edna can't keep her mouth shut.'

Shane finished his can and slumped back into his chair. He patted his stomach and grinned. 'I could get used to this life. You can't beat a good Chin—' A look of fear settled in his eyes, intensifying as he sat up.

Renee straightened. 'What's wrong now?'

'I just remembered that Pete-the-Chink's car is parked around the back. Mich said she'd call him and tell him where it was.'

Renee grimaced at the mention of Mich's name. 'Even when that bitch isn't here, she's still causing us problems.'

Shane stood up and walked over to the window. There was a distant look in his eyes as though his mind was someplace else.

'Shane,' Renee said. 'Shane?' She said his name three more times before he answered.

'Huh?'

'What's wrong with you?'

He walked over to the table and grabbed a can, flicked back the lid, and took three huge swigs. He swigged some more, crushing the can in his hand after he'd emptied it. Using the back of his hand, he wiped the residue from his lips, then stared down at the linoleum covered floor.

Renee stood up and rested a hand on his shoulder. Shane brushed it off, and by the look on his face, there was no consoling him.

'Shane,' she said. 'Shane, speak to me. What's wrong?'

He scowled at her. 'Are you stupid or something? I thought that was obvious.'

'You mean that Pete fella's car?'

'Of course, I mean his car. What else would I be talking about?'

'All right, no need to shout.'

Shane raked his thick, nicotine-stained fingers through

his hair. He caught Jay's glance. 'And what the hell are you gawping at?'

Renee stood between them. 'This has nothing to do with Jay. Don't you take it out on him.'

Shane covered his face with his hands and breathed deeply. He dropped his hands to his sides. 'What are we going to do? That Pete fella's going to come for his car sooner or later.'

Renee shook her head. 'I doubt that. He would have been here by now, probably doesn't even know where it is.'

'Mich might have told him.'

'I don't think so. The bitch was too busy running away.'

Shane grabbed another can.

Renee sighed. 'That's really going to help.'

'Don't start, woman.'

'Well stop drinking then.'

Jay wondered how long it would take them to kick off. Things were quiet for too long and he knew it wouldn't last. When Shane started drinking, even the smoothest of days cracked.

Jay slipped outside and stood in the garden, facing the trees, his back turned to their bawling. It was darker now, the sky, the trees, and the fields muted beneath a veil of inky blue. He glimpsed something in the distance, a spark, a flame, a flash of torchlight. He wasn't sure what it was, so took a closer look. Jay shoved his hands into his pockets and headed towards the dip of hills beyond the trees.

3

DON'T FEAR THE REAPER

If the bullet had been half an inch lower, it would have struck Nash's brain. Instead, it burned across his scalp, like a streak of fiery liquid grabbing chunks of skin and hair in its wake. Blood masked his face, filled his eyes until all he saw was a hazy, white light. He'd never experienced such pain. It was like a knife twisting through the top of his skull, intensifying as his legs weakened, forcing him to fall backwards and crack his head against the ivy-covered stones.

Luckily, Shane had never buried a man before, so there was no reason he should do it right: he'd dug the grave too shallow, the peaty earth barely covering Nash's body and enabling him to breathe. It was a poor excuse for a grave, a frightened man's panicked fumbling. Yet Nash was grateful for such ineptitude. He felt blessed even, lying there on his back, wiping the dust from his eyes, spitting the dirt out.

IT WASN'T the first time Nash had risen from the dead. There had been all that mess with young Frankie Hilditch, and the bigger mess that followed. Since that time Nash was a changed man, although most would have described him as 'broken'. He didn't care. None of them had a clue. They embraced the parts they wanted to believe and indulged their imaginations for the rest. But he learned to live with that. The tale of Frankie Hilditch leaving him for dead sat more comfortably than the truth.

How long had it been? Fifteen? Twelve? Ten years at least. He met Hilditch in the sixties. The kid's keenness struck him. He carried a crazy glint in his eyes. Living his life with his foot always on the gas, sooner or later he was bound to burn himself out.

Against his better judgment, Nash let Hilditch in on a small con. The kid had been a petty thief up until then and viewed the job as his big break, grinning throughout each planning session, thanking Nash continually, telling him he was forever grateful.

Once the job was over, Hilditch's gratitude proved as fickle as his temper. In the subsequent weeks, he became convinced Nash short-changed him, underpaid him for his services. His grievances grew more vocal, sharing his contempt for Nash throughout the clubs and pubs with all and sundry. He didn't appear to care who he told. All that mattered was that they listened. He didn't even need a sympathetic ear.

Hilditch's grievances quickly turned into threats. Dissatisfied, it seemed, with telling the same old story, the kid decreed to turn his words into action. Nash was out of town so Hilditch went to find him. They crossed paths one drizzly, autumn afternoon in Whitstable. Nash went there to rest, spending his days between drinking in various pubs and walking along the deserted coastline. On a desolate stretch of sand, Hilditch blocked Nash's way. The kid looked phantom-like standing there in the half mist. Anger ignited his eyes. Beads of water glistened on his hair, the pale, ash-grey hues of his skin stressing his five o'clock shadow.

Yet the deception was momentary. The light's trickery evaporated, exposing a young man in a loose-fitting suit, his trouser bottoms laden with wet sand and his white cotton shirt soaked through, an interloper standing incongruently between the land and the sea.

'What the hell do *you* want?' Nash asked although he knew the answer.

Hilditch made his demands. The kid spoke too quickly and appeared fidgety.

Nash tried reasoning with him and in doing so attempted to get into the kid's head, get to the root of his anger. Yet Hilditch's sense of injustice took him beyond compromise. The young man remained furious, demanding a bigger cut and greater credit for his part in it.

Nash realised the kid wanted more than that. He boasted about it for weeks: how he needed to teach Nash a lesson. The kid wasn't angry about money. He might have convinced himself that was the case. But all he wanted was respect, to make a name for himself, and Nash was his means to that all-important reputation.

Hilditch's hand shook as he gripped the leather cosh. At least he intended to leave Nash alive: the crippled quarry and sole witness to his story. Nash remembered thinking how naive Hilditch was. If you wanted to hurt a man, the last thing you did was give him a warning.

The instant Hilditch raised his hand, Nash's instincts kicked in. He aimed his punch at the kid's jaw but smashed his fist straight into his soft windpipe. Hilditch fell to his knees and clasped his bony fingers around his throat. He looked strange kneeling there, like a sea creature suddenly finding itself washed ashore, gaping, wheezing, its eyes wide with disbelief.

Nash tried to save him, loosening the lad's shirt, giving him mouth to mouth. Such a frightening way to die, suffocation, the eyes raised, that desperate fight for breath.

Reliving it after all this time was like watching a dream within a dream, and Nash, the voyeur of his own and someone else's slow death. Nash saw himself laden Hilditch's pockets with stones. Watched himself drag Hilditch's body into the water. All kinds of strange stories riddled the weeks following Hilditch's death. Some said Nash was dead, coshed to a pulp, giving Hilditch everything he owned in a last, desperate plea for his life. There were sightings of Hilditch, brief exchanges in French hotels, backroom card games, and drunken brawls in the Costa del Sol.

In the months that followed it became apparent that Nash wasn't dead, although the man who returned was an imposter, a dispirited apparition of his former self. Nash spread the rumours, using Hilditch's name throughout his travels, and to this day it remained his greatest con. But his demeanour was the most convincing. The change was real. No one could have maintained such an act for that long. It was as though Hilditch's shadow constantly followed him, weakened his smile, dulled the glint in his eyes. Mostly, he managed not to think about it. But there remained a heaviness inside him, which, combined with the guilt he felt for his granddad and Danny Greer, made it difficult not to be a changed man, a man haunted by so many ghosts.

As NASH LAY in his makeshift grave, he'd seen the old man standing over him. Watching him like he used to, with a discerning look on his face. Nash reached out his hand.

But the old man refused it, tut-tutting with disapproval before ordering him to stand. Nash barely managed to sit up. His legs were dead weights. His head throbbed. His arms shook as he pushed himself up from the soil. He sat trembling. He could feel water inside his mouth and a shot of bile travelled up his throat. He tried to swallow as little as he could, spitting it out, feeling it dribble down his chin.

He heard the old man's voice in his head. 'You dirty bastard. You were like that when you were a little kid.'

'I can't help it,' Nash mumbled.

He pictured the old man's toothless grin, heard a pitiful voice say, 'I know. I understand. I was the same when I was dying in the hospital.'

Nash mustered a defeated sigh. 'I should have been there, taken care of you.'

He saw the old man's fierce glare. 'Yes, you should have. But what's done is done.'

Behind his closed eyelids, Nash saw flashes of orange light. 'I'm sorry,' he said.

A coldness passed across his shoulders. 'It's partly my fault,' said a familiar voice. 'But we can remedy that. Don't sit here in the dirt with blood all over you. These things you chase, they're for fools and dogs. This is no life, Nash. You can come back with me if you like.'

Something warm stirred in his stomach, travelled through his veins. His limbs lightened, the warmth intensified, easing his pain, and spreading across his chest.

The notion tempted him. The thought of being with his grandfather triggered something inside him. A sense of release took hold of him. He felt calmer, more fulfilled. Such a wondrous feeling, like those hazed, moments of blissful solitude between wakefulness and sleep. For a moment, he embraced the feeling and almost succumbed to it. Then the pain returned, forcing his eyes open.

The harsh afternoon light fired Nash's senses. It pressed him to stand, reminded him his time wasn't over yet. It urged him forward, one slow step at a time.

Don't you dare stop, said the voice inside. *Not until you've taken back what was stolen.*

NASH STAGGERED down the overgrown path. He stumbled a few times, holding onto the adjacent hedgerows. The thorns pierced his fingers.

He scoured the road for his car. Then the image of Mich pointing the gun at him flashed through his mind, and he realised she'd taken it.

He ambled along the pavement, his head down, trying not to attract attention. A few cars beeped as they passed but Nash didn't look up.

When he reached the sign for the Swimming Baths, he crossed the road and followed the hill towards town. In the public toilets, he washed the blood from his face and hands.

For a moment, he stared into the cracked, graffitied mirror. He couldn't believe the man looking back was him. The face was deathly pale. A streak of congealed blood ran through his hair. A film of broken skin coated his bottom lip. Dark shadows circled his eyes making them appear more sunken.

He caught the Sunday market just as they were packing up, and with the crumpled twenty he found in his back pocket, he bought a cheap, white t-shirt. The stallholder watched as Nash put it on. The bemused look on the man's face turning into laughter when Nash chucked his bloodied shirt into the bin.

'Have you been in a fight, mate?' the man said.

Nash strained a smile. 'Something like that.'

The man studied him for a second. 'You want to get yourself to the Cottage Hospital. You don't look well, mate. You don't sound too handy either.'

Nash carried on up the high street. He sensed every passer-by either glance or stare at him. He didn't return one look, even when someone asked if he was all right.

Nash felt weaker now, and every step was a strain. The gash on his head hurt like hell, smarting beneath the sun, seeming deeper with every touch. He stopped every few minutes to catch his breath, wipe the sweat from his brow.

Death's brief encounter aged him, weakened his bones, returned him to this scorched, arid land as an old man. Nash fastened on the image of his granddad, wondering if the vision was more than a dream. He'd always heard the old man's voice, only this time it was clearer. What would have happened, he wondered, if he followed his granddad into the trees? The answer stopped him in his tracks, a pang of anxiety wrenched in his stomach at the sudden realisation that he'd almost succumbed to death.

Nash cast the thought aside and continued to Jay's house. It was the only place he could think of. Perhaps Jay and his mam were still there? Maybe Shane had left with Mich? He smiled at the thought. It was a foolish notion. Mich wouldn't have gone anywhere with Shane. Pete probably had more chance. For the first time in Nash's life, Pete had a use. He had a car, could help him track down Mich. Pete had worked things out. He didn't need to ask any questions.

When Nash arrived at the house, he leaned against the gate to catch his breath. In all the time he'd known Jay and his mam, he'd never seen the place so quiet. It seemed different somehow. Usually, there was at least one window open, the sound of the TV or radio blaring out into the street. Today all the windows were shut. The curtains were half drawn. Shane's van was missing, too. An unnatural silence loitered over the house, a loneliness even, like most things which had been abandoned.

As Nash opened the gate, Edna, the next-door neighbour, popped her head out of her bedroom window. He'd met her a few times, but she stared at him as though he were a stranger. 'They're on holiday, won't be back until next week.'

'Do you know where they've gone?'

She opened her mouth to say something, hesitated for a second, then said, 'Up the tops. You know, Shane's bungalow.'

Nash nodded, a sudden tiredness forcing him to close his eyes. He broke into a cold sweat. A sound like a distant bell chimed in his ears. Saliva filled his mouth. A heavy, sickly feeling rooted in the pit of his stomach.

He rested on his haunches and retched. Pain throbbed in his head, dulled his senses until there was only darkness.

When he opened his eyes, he was sitting on the pavement, his back resting against the hedge. Edna stood in front of him holding a glass of water. A couple of kids stopped to watch.

Edna crouched down and offered him the glass. 'Are you all right, love? What have you done to your head? You look awful.'

Nash took the glass from her and took a sip. The cold water burned against the rawness of his throat. He coughed. Then held out his hand, in reaction to the worried look on Edna's face, to tell her he was all right. He pressed the chilled glass against his forehead, relished the sensation for a few seconds, then got up. His legs felt drained of strength and he gripped the hedge to balance himself, flashing a smile of gratitude as Edna held his arm.

'Come inside for a minute,' she said.

He let her guide him into the house, willingly playing the part of the wounded soldier. He slumped into the sofa, keeping his eyes open, knowing if he closed them, they would stay shut.

The room was sparser than he'd expected. The air fresheners and the open windows couldn't hide the smell of cigarettes. Edna offered him a cup of tea, but Nash shook his head. 'No thanks, do you have any painkillers?'

She disappeared into the kitchen, coming back into the room a few minutes later with a fresh glass of water and a half box of Co-Codamol. She threw the tablets onto his lap and placed the drink at his feet. 'You can keep those. I've got another box.'

He took out four tablets, popped them in his mouth, washing them down with a huge swig of water. He emptied the glass, then wiped the residue from his lips. 'Thanks. I can't wait for these to kick in.'

Edna pointed at the gash on his head. 'You should get that seen to. How on earth did you manage it?'

'Running through the woods, caught it on a branch.'

'Is that right? You must have been moving pretty fast then.'

Nash glanced at her telephone. 'Sorry to trouble you further, but could I call a taxi?'

'Blexies are the best.' She gave him the number. 'Don't forget to put ten pence in the box.'

Edna had one of those new Trimphones like the one on *The Golden Shot*. Nash dialled the number and after two rings a woman answered. She sounded sluggish and pissed off, a combination of the heat and a bad attitude. 'Can I have taxi please from twenty-four Moor Hill . . . As quick as you can...Afonwen... Past the woods... I'll show the driver when I get there... And how much is that?... Okay, thank you.'

He hung up, threw Edna a smile before dropping a handful of change into her wooden money box.

'Thanks for your kindness,' he said. 'Once I sort a few things out, I'll see you right.'

'And what things are those? Are you going to get even with that tree?'

Nash nodded and smiled. 'Yeah, something like that.'

IN THE BACK of the taxi, Nash's eyes fixed on the passing scenery. The tablets started working, suppressing the pain to a dull ache. If only they'd shut out the sound, he thought, and stop the driver from rabbiting on about the state of the country. Nash hardly said a word. The only time he spoke was when he asked the driver to stop at a garage where he bought four packs of cigarettes, a disposable lighter, and a load of chocolate bars and crisps. He was ravenous and ate as much as he could.

As they approached the sign that said Afonwen, Nash asked the driver to stop. It seemed an odd location for a sign: placed alongside a narrow country lane that was almost a dirt track. It was surrounded by woods and fields. Pot-bellied hills loomed in the distance.

Nash handed the driver his fare. 'How far is the village?'

The driver frowned. 'What village? There's no village here, mate. There's a craft centre half a mile ahead. The rest is houses. I think there might be a pub and a shop.'

Nash gestured for him to keep the change. 'I haven't been up here for years. I want to surprise an old friend of mine. He lives around here somewhere in a yellow bungalow.'

The driver pointed to where the lane dipped from sight and a row of hedges marked the outline of a steep hill. 'The only yellow bungalow I know of is up there. But that place has been abandoned for ages.'

Nash opened the rear door. 'No worries, I'll take my chances.'

'I'll drive you up there if you want?'

'Nah, I fancy the walk.'

'Are you sure you're up to it? It's a good climb you know.'

'I'll be fine,' Nash said and got out the car, gently closing the door behind him.

As NASH SLOGGED his way up the hill, it felt as though he'd lost something. A part of himself gone forever, something strong replaced by a weakness that ate away at him. Whatever it was, this thing turned his legs to jelly, aged him before his years. He grew more breathless with every step, sweat oozing from every pore. His head throbbed. The nape of his back ached as though an angel of death pressed down on his shoulders.

He saw the bungalow when he was only halfway up, and a tinge of hope touched his heart at the sight of Shane's van parked in the driveway.

This was as far as he could go for now. He was in no fit state to do anything. He needed rest, get his strength back to put things right. He turned around and headed back towards the lane, stopping when he came across a stile. It took all his strength to climb over it. A burgeoning feeling of relief accompanied him as he stepped into the field. He strolled along the bank, followed it to the dried-up stream, then hunkered down, resting beneath the shade of the trees.

NASH LAY THERE FOR HOURS. Drifting in and out of sleep. Listening to the birds' faint chatter undulate through the trees. It was late evening. A low sun loomed, darkening the fields with shadow.

The persistent throb in his head was almost blinding. His stomach growled. A dull ache stiffened his bones. He should have felt better than this. He didn't even feel rested. Then something stirred in the grass. Nash flicked back his lighter and saw the brown, shocked face of a boy glowing behind the flame.

4

WILD IS THE WIND

Except in the films, Jay hadn't seen a ghost. He longed to. But the closest he ever came to it was in his dreams. Perhaps he was dreaming now, the thud of his heart, the churning in his stomach nothing more than an illusion. Nash's pale corpse stood in front of him, held him spellbound, and, as Jay was about to cry out, placed a hand over his mouth.

'Don't be frightened,' the spectre whispered. 'It's me Jay. Nash. The bullet grazed me. I didn't die.'

It sounded like Nash. The voice a little more sluggish perhaps, but Nash's voice all the same. The hand felt real too: warm and sweaty, thick fingers covered with rough skin. For a second, Jay had half a mind to bite into it but reconsidered for fear of retaliation.

'I'm sorry to frighten you,' Nash said. He laughed to himself. 'To be honest, bud, I don't know who was more scared, you or me.' He lowered his voice. 'I'm going to move my hand away now. But you need to promise me you won't scream, shout for help, or run off.'

Jay nodded, taking a deep breath the moment Nash released him. He remained silent, the spike of fear in the pit of his stomach diminishing slightly. Yet he could still feel the rapid beat of his heart.

It felt strange standing there. Nash was alive but by the look of him only just. He was pale, his eyes bloodshot. The gash on his head looked like something from a Hammer horror movie. There was something odd about the way Nash spoke, too, and as he told Jay what happened, his speech sounded slurry, each word drawn out as though there was something lodged in the corner of his mouth.

'Have you come for the money?' Jay said.

Nash sat down on the bank. 'Yeah, but not all of it. I'll still see you and your mam right. I promised you that.'

Jay smiled and sat beside him. He listened to the heaviness of Nash's breath and felt the heat radiate from his skin. Stars twinkled in the half darkness, and the smell of scorched grass filled the air. Every few minutes or so, Jay heard the sudden rush of a car, saw a flash of headlights through the hedgerows. Except for that, it was mostly silent.

Jay watched Nash's hand tremble as he lit his cigarette. He didn't like to see his friend look so vulnerable and that familiar feeling of sadness weighed inside him.

Nash smiled. As though reading Jay's mind he said, 'Cheer up, bud.'

'I'm fine, was just thinking.'

Nash shuffled closer. 'About what?'

'Shane...You should have seen the way he acted when he thought you were dead.'

'Scared, huh?'

'The dickhead shit himself.'

Nash tried to laugh, but he broke into a cough. He kept

thumping his chest until the coughing eased, then closed his eyes for an instant, took a deep breath. 'Don't make me laugh, bud.' He wiped the tears from his eyes. 'That's no surprise. Shane's full of crap. I should have told you that from the start.' He rested a hand on Jay's shoulder. 'Mich took all the money, right?'

Jay shook his head.

'Really? How much did she leave him?'

'About a third. A bit more than that, perhaps. There's at least ten thousand.'

'Phew. I bet he's keeping a close eye on that?'

'He's getting pissed at the moment, arguing with Mam. He still thinks the money's under the bed.'

Nash beamed. 'But you've hidden it, right?'

Jay nodded. 'I'll teach him not to pick on me. Anyway, it's not his. He never earned it. He was squawking like a big baby at first, told Mam some bullshit, begging her to believe him, then started going back to his old, horrible self.'

Nash nodded. 'He's feeling more confident. Thinks he's going to get away with it.'

'He was until he remembered that Pete fella.'

'What about him?'

'His car's still at the house. Shane's worried he's gonna come back for it. I don't know why. If he were gonna come, he would have come for it by now.'

Nash removed his hand from Jay's shoulder. 'Pete came to the bungalow?'

'No, Mich drove the car there.'

Nash pressed the heels of his hands into the grass and pushed himself up. Jay got up too, the worried look in Nash's eyes making him feel uneasy.

'Don't you go near that car, Jay. Jay? Do hear me?'

Jay nodded, watching in silence while Nash staggered over to a tree and rested against it.

Nash was breathing more heavily now, a brush of moonlight lit part of his face, revealing the dark circles around his eyes and the lines across his ashen skin. He bowed his head slightly and spat into the grass. A thin, strand of saliva glistened across his bottom lip.

'Are you all right?' Jay said. 'You look like you need some rest.'

'I'll get plenty of rest later. After we've sorted things out.' He flashed Jay a weak smile. 'Are you up for that, bud?'

Jay nodded.

'Good lad. I knew I could rely on you.' He slowly raised his arm and beckoned Jay closer, then let it fall to his side. Sweat trickled from his brow. His throat crackled with each breath. He fumbled in his pocket and pulled out a pack of cigarettes. He tried popping one into his mouth but dropped it on the grass.

Jay crouched down, picked it up, and handed it back.

'Thanks,' Nash said. 'Blasted thing slipped through my fingers.' He placed it behind his ear. 'I'll smoke it later.' He threw Jay a wink. 'Don't worry about me. I'll be okay. It looks worse than what it is.'

Jay knew that wasn't true but didn't answer. Instead, he forced a smile and stepped forward. He felt awkward, fixed his eyes on the ground, not knowing where to look. When he raised his head, Nash was staring at him. 'Right,' Nash said, lowering his voice as though somebody might listen, 'this is what I want you to do.' He pointed in the house's direction. 'You need to bring me the money, a bit of food, and Shane's van keys if you can.'

'What about Mam?'

'Don't say anything just yet. Let me sort it.'

Jay gave him a wary look.

'Don't worry, bud. You can trust me. I won't let you down again.' He studied Jay for a second, then let out a laugh.

'What's so funny?' Jay said.

'Me; these woods; the night; giving you a list of things to fetch. We're like Magwitch and Pip, you know, from *Great Expectations*.'

'I suppose,' Jay said. But it didn't feel like that. It was scary, kind of sad even.

'You don't have to do any of this, Jay, if you don't want to. I just think the money, you and your mam will be better off with me. Sounds to me like Shane's planning on taking it anyway.'

'I want to do it. That money belongs to you.'

'And you've earned your share of it.' He ruffled Jay's hair. 'You best go now. Your mam will wonder where've you got to.'

Jay doubted that. She was probably still arguing with Shane, hadn't even noticed he'd gone. He didn't tell Nash that. He nodded, turned around, and made his way back up the hill. He glanced over his shoulder every couple of minutes, part of him still wondering if it was a dream, a feeling of emptiness growing inside him as Nash faded into the distance.

LIGHT SPILLED out from the open doorway, yellowing the scorched grass and brightening the path. Jay paused at the gate and stared through the kitchen window. There was no sign of his mam nor Shane. A choir sang a hymn on the radio. Jay's heart sank at the sound of it and was reminded of those dread-filled Sunday nights before school. Begrudgingly, he shoved open the gate and tiptoed up the path.

Something didn't feel right. Jay wasn't sure what, but it forced him to creep into the hallway.

Once inside, he heard Shane, swearing, and rummaging through drawers from what sounded like the back bedroom. He felt the urge to call out for his mam. Instead, he lowered his breath and stepped slowly into the kitchen. She was sitting on the floor, slumped against the fridge, one eye swollen and closed, blood smeared across her mouth. Fearing one day he would find her like this, Jay always tried to be ready for it. Yet nothing could prepare him. The reality was more frightening. He crouched beside her, placed a hand on her forehead. 'Mam,' he whispered. 'Mam, are you all right?'

She opened her eyes, gave a faint smile, and cried. 'Oh, Jay, what have you done with that money, love? Shane's going mental.' She squeezed his arm. 'Run to the phone box, call the police.'

Jay considered it for a second. 'No, Mam. I need to stay with you. I can't leave you like this.'

A door slammed, then, as though a wild animal were charging through the house, Jay heard heavy footsteps bolting along the hall. His first instinct was to run. But he just stood there. Afraid, yes, but not grounded by fear. No, he remained there to protect his mam.

As Shane entered the kitchen, Renee pushed herself up. She staggered forward, blocking his way. 'You leave him alone. You leave him alone.' She sounded hoarse, breathless, was wobbly on her feet, and Jay touched her arm, fearing she might collapse.

'Oh, I'll leave him alone all right,' Shane said. 'Once I've skinned the little bastard. I'll teach him to take the piss out of me.' He tried shoving Renee aside, but she refused to budge, grabbing a fistful of his hair, pulling his head towards her as she dropped to her knees.

Shane shrieked in pain. He appeared immobilised for a second, then grabbed Renee's throat, squeezing hard until she released him. She slumped onto her side, coughing, tears streaming down her face. As Jay tried to help her, Shane grabbed him around the waist and slung him over his shoulder. He carried him into the hall, Jay's kicking and punching having little effect. It was as though he was weightless, a bundle of cheap rags.

A feeling of helplessness rushed through Jay's body as Shane carried him outside. He cried out for his mam, and in the silence that followed, he thought of Nash. So what if he'd risen from the dead? He was no help to him now. He may as well be a ghost.

Jay cried out for his mam again, only this time it wasn't a feeling of powerlessness that silenced him, but Shane clacking him across the back of the head.

Shane slipped Jay off his shoulder and started leading him by the arm. 'Stop your whining,' he said. He dragged him to the rear end of the abandoned car, gripping his wrist with his right hand while using his left to open the boot. A foul smell filled the air, a mix of sweat, heat, and shit, the devil's brew topped with the summer's pestilence.

Jay gagged, vomiting a mouthful of bile and spit as Shane pulled him closer.

Jay thought it was a dog for a second, covered with a man's bloody shirt. He soon realised what it was. The body of the man he'd met down the estuary, Nash's friend, Pete. He was slumped on his side, hands between his legs, with his mouth and eyes wide open. It was an ungodly sight, a man lost between wakefulness and sleep.

Jay hoped he wouldn't die like that, forgotten and abandoned. He tried to look away, but Shane pushed his face closer.

'You take a good look,' Shane said. 'I caught him sniffing around, cut his throat clean open.' He grabbed Jay's hair and yanked his head back. 'You tell me where that money is, or the same thing's gonna happen to you.'

Tears streamed down Jay's cheeks, and although he was frightened, all he could think about was his mam. 'Get off me. Get off me. I'll tell ya once we've phoned for an ambulance.'

Shane pulled Jay's hair tighter. 'You're in no position to bargain. Tell me, you little shite. Come on, don't make me ask you again.'

Jay pointed at the gate. 'It's over there.'

'Where?'

'By the lane, I buried it under the grass.'

Shane released Jay's hair and gave him a shove. 'You better not be lying.' He shoved him again. 'Come on, show me, dig it up.'

Jay's arm hurt like hell as Shane marched him down the path. A rawness grated inside his throat, and his t-shirt clung to this sweaty skin. He kept glancing over his shoulder, checking for his mam. There was no sign of her. Not a sound. For all he knew, she was dead. He tried reasoning with Shane again, but Shane wasn't having it.

'Shut it. You get me that money. You'll see her soon enough.'

Jay was too scared to answer. He just focused on the lane ahead. So many things rushed through his mind: Why had Shane hurt Mam? Was it because Jay hid the money, or because Shane killed Pete? Perhaps Mam tried to stop him, call the police?

They followed the grass verge along the adjacent lane,

slowly, until Jay saw a small mound of soil and stopped. 'I think it's here somewhere.'

'You think? You only buried it a few hours ago.'

'It was dark.'

'Yeah, well now it's darker.' He gave Jay a shove almost pushing him over. 'You've got ten minutes. You better pray that you find it.'

Jay rested on his haunches. There was no use praying. God hadn't helped him so far. He took a deep breath. An anxious feeling rolled in his stomach. His heart beat in his throat as he considered whether to make a run for it.

He grabbed a handful of soil, held it in his fist.

'What are you staring into space for?' Shane said.

'I'm not. I'm thinking.'

Before Shane could answer, Jay slung the soil into his eyes just like he'd seen in the movies. Then he stood up, punched him in the groin, and, without checking to see if any of this had an effect, ran. He darted towards the woods, breaking into a sprint, his pace faltering slightly as he zigzagged between the trees.

Jay didn't dare look behind him, knowing that if he did, it would slow him down, allowing Shane to catch him. By the sound of it, he was only a hair's breadth away. Something heavy crunched through the grass and he heard the heaviness of each breath behind him. Jay kept running, expecting that any second now Shane's big, sweaty hand would grab his shoulder, and pull him to the ground, then cut his belly open or something much worse, abandoning him among the deadness of the trees.

As the woods petered out, Jay could see the narrow B-road below and the brow of the hill beyond it where Nash waited for him by the dried-out stream. He just needed to keep running. He was almost there now. His legs weakened.

A razor-sharp pain burned inside his chest. Running downhill proved more arduous than sprinting across the flats. The thud of each step shot up through his back, almost buckling his knees. He glanced over his shoulder to see where Shane was, checking the distance between them.

Shane was closer than he'd hoped, gaining ground now and showing no signs of tiring.

Shane went wide, running alongside Jay, trying to reach the gate before him. Jay considered running straight towards the hedge and climbing over it. No, it was too high. Shane would grab him before he reached the top. The gate was his only chance. He'd have to clear it quickly, though, sprint across the road, leap over the stile.

As Jay climbed over the gate, he heard the words 'Got you!' For a second he thought all was lost, until he saw Nash on the opposite side of the road, sitting on the grass verge with his back against the hedge. Jay didn't notice the car as he sprinted across the road. All he heard was a loud thud behind him and the piercing screech of tyres as it braked.

The young woman who rushed out of the car paid no attention to Jay. Instead, she knelt beside Shane's body and held his hand, her shoulders shaking. 'I'm so sorry,' she kept saying. She turned to face Jay, sobbing between each breath. 'I slowed down for him. I thought he was going to run straight across. He just stopped in the middle of the road.'

Jay looked at Nash, wondering why he was still slumped against the hedge. There had been an accident. Nash needed to take control of the situation. 'Hey, Nash,' Jay shouted. 'This lady needs help. Shane's been hit.'

Nash didn't answer, he remained still, his body breathless as Jay stared into the cold deadness of his eyes.

In the years to follow, Jay would think of this moment often. He would picture Shane, chasing after him, on the cusp of triumph. The cocksure look in his eyes snapped out like a candle flame as he stared at what he believed to be the Nash's ghost. Then, with tears in his eyes, and the knot in his stomach tightening, Jay would picture his old friend. Nash deserved better than that, he'd tell himself, until the fear and the cold silenced him and he wondered what it was like to die alone.

EPILOGUE

J ay stayed with his auntie Bev while his mam recovered in hospital. He didn't realise at the time that he'd end up living with Bev for a while. His mam needed to recover and there was all that trouble with the social services.

Bev lived in northwest Wales, in a small town called Barmouth, by the sea. There were fewer people there. Tourists mostly, their numbers dwindling as summer ended. The official report read that the drought would last another six weeks. Then, in September, the rain came. The wettest month since World War II. Days before they'd been rationing water. The councils didn't have a clue. It was a lucky dip, depending on where you lived. One side of the street would have water while the other would have their supply cut off, resentment running rife among neighbouring avenues and streets.

At first, most people in the town seemed grateful for the rain. But as the days dragged on, Jay noticed a different kind of talk as he roamed the town and its streets. There was a hint of longing in their voices as they spoke of those warm summer nights, and a glint in their eyes as they recalled what now seemed a distant memory. And although Jay felt that same, he didn't mind getting wet. In fact, some days he even liked it, wiping the rain from his eyes, relishing its cold kiss against his skin.

His auntie Bev didn't like him walking in the rain. *You look like a drowned rat*, she'd say. *Dry yourself, quickly now, before you catch pneumonia.* He didn't mind her going on at him. He enjoyed the fuss.

Every day until the end of the summer holidays, Jay took the same route. Starting from his auntie Bev's house, he'd take a left down Dewi Avenue, walk up the long, steep Bryn Mawr Hill, and saunter into town. He'd kill a bit of time in Woolies, flicking through album covers, stealing sweets from the pick 'n mix. Then he'd make his way along the prom and down to the beach.

He spent hours along the shore, longer if the tide was out. When the rain became too heavy, he took shelter beneath one of the old gazebos, gazing across the sand, taking deep breaths to subdue the sadness. He thought mostly about his mam, wondered if she'd ever be the same. He dreaded those weekly visits to the hospital. The journey was too long. His mam complained and worried about everything or burst into tears and told him how sorry she was. She'd hug him when it was time to leave. 'You keep that money safe, Jay,' she'd whisper. 'It'll be all right as long as we keep shtum.'

The news about Nash, Shane, and Nash's friend Pete was in all the national papers. There was a story about it on the TV too. The police questioned Jay and his mam for days until they were convinced their stories matched. Jay didn't say a thing at first. But the police kept on at him until he finally gave in. He told them everything, and when they asked him about Pete's body, he told them he didn't have a clue. As far he knew, Shane killed him, and they seemed satisfied with that. And when he showed them where the money was, they bought him fish and chips and told him he was 'a good lad'.

'All this for just a thousand-bloody quid,' the inspector said. Only this time, Jay never said a thing.

Remembering that scene always reminded him of Nash. If Jay ever thought about his old friend while he was on the shore, he'd grab a handful of pebbles and skim them across the sand. It provided a brief respite. But once those memories took root, the sadness in Jay's heart was overwhelming. Sometimes the darkest thoughts plagued his mind, loneliness and loss, the cruel finality of death.

As he made his way home, sometimes he'd take a shortcut through the park. He came across the same gang of boys now and then. Some of them were his age, others were a bit older. They tried intimidating him at first. But Jay had learned from the master and soon put a stop to that.

When he was around those boys, he didn't act like himself. He took on a new persona, his mannerisms, voice, and words emulating Nash. It didn't take long to have the desired effect. Those boys soon started calling him by his first name, inviting him over whenever he walked past, offering him a can of beer and the odd cigarette.

Jay only ever took a sip, kept the cigarettes for Bev, just doing enough to convince them.

Sometimes, when he got home, he'd hand Bev a quid, or an almost full pack of cigarettes, and tell her he found it on the street. He always left a few weeks between each gift; he'd learned to be clever the hard way.

As time went on, he stopped dreaming about that

perfect house. He still had enough money to buy one, but he'd other plans for it now. He needed to look after Bev and his mam. And, when he was old enough, he needed to find Mich, not for him, but for Nash.

AFTERWORD

Thanks for reading. If you **enjoyed this book,** please consider leaving **a review**. Reviews make a huge difference in helping new readers find the book.

Building a relationship with readers is the best thing about writing.

Join Math Bird's readers' list for information on new books and release dates **www.mathbird.uk**

Check out the first book in the
Ned Flynn *Crime Thriller Series*
THE WHISTLING SANDS

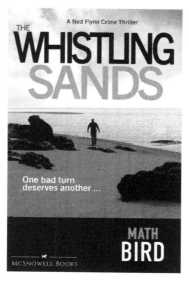

*A good woman can be the making of a man, a bad one can
lead to ruin . . . Distraught ex-con Ned Flynn desperately
needs cash to support his frail mother, but currently he's
broke. When a local entrepreneur offers him cash to find his
runaway wife, Nia, Flynn sees little choice.*

COMING SOON

Hidden Grace

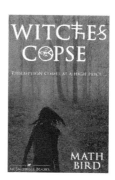

Witches Copse

ABOUT THE AUTHOR

Math Bird is a British novelist and short story writer.

He's a member of the Crime Writers Association, and his work has aired on BBC Radio 4, Radio Wales, and Radio 4 Extra.

For more information: www.mathbird.uk